The Proposal
By
Jaden Sinclair

Published by
Melange Books, LLC
White Bear Lake, MN 55110
www.melange-books.com

ISBN **978-1-61235-036-3**
The Proposal - Jaden Sinclair, Copyright © 2010, 2011

Credits

Editor: Nancy Schumacher
Copy Editor: Taylor Evans
Format Editor: Mae Powers
Cover Artist: A. Bratt

The Proposal
By
Jaden Sinclair

Nathaniel Remington is rich, smart, gorgeous, and very lonely—always doing the right thing expected of him, never listening to his heart. For years he's held on to a hidden desire—a woman he could never have, but always wanted.

Danielle Hughes has shouldered her family burdens for a long time. When fate hits with another blow, Danielle is at a loss. Nathaniel steps in, offering her a proposition she considers. Can she accept spending two weeks in his arms, or will she lose everything in his seductive proposal?

Dedication

For all the girls out there who think that your knight in shinning armor isn't out there; he is.

www.jadensinclair.com

Interplanetary Passions
Outerplanetary Sensations
Shifters 1-7
S.E.T.H.
S.H.I.L.O.
Lucifer's Lust, with Mae Powers

The Proposal
By
Jaden Sinclair

Chapter One

Danielle Hughes sat at the break table at the back of her fast food job, frowning over the little book she held in her hand. Going over the figures in her savings account book, she tried to think of a way she could pay for her first semester of college. Half of her paycheck always went to her family, mostly toward her brother's medical bills. Paul Hughes, her older brother, and the light in her father's eyes, was dying. He needed a new liver and they didn't have the money to pay for the operation, even if a donor could be found.

Ever since Paul got sick, it was up to Danielle to work and help with the bills. Her father's first and only concern was for Paul. Even her mother acted like she was just a small bank they could withdraw money from at will. Another thing starting to take its toll on Danielle was her hidden college funds. Balances were starting to go down instead of up. Then to put the icing on the cake, her hours were going to be cut.

Danielle Hughes stood at only five three. Her build wasn't that of a slim super model, but a nice size fourteen. Her soft, wavy dirty blonde hair she kept cut to her shoulders in layers around her face. Her soft, pouty lips seemed to scream, 'kiss me!' But her green eyes that once reflected the carefree life of youth, now showed the burden of family.

At one time, Danielle even thought of herself as pretty, before she started to look older than her young twenty-two years. She had only been seventeen when Paul became sick, and as far as she was concerned, her youth was gone. The one and only boyfriend that she ever had broke up with her after her father's demands became too much. Then after high school, all of her friends stopped coming around when they kept getting turned down because of the duties her father inflicted upon her. All in all, when Paul got sick, Danielle disappeared.

"Thought your shift was up," her boss said, walking back with some books in her hands.

"It is. Just thinking how I'm going to explain to my father why we're cutting back on hours."

"I'm sure he'll understand."

Danielle put her book back in her purse and stood up. "I don't think so."

Instead of heading home and facing her father, Danielle changed her clothes in the back of her beat up Tempo and headed for the hospital. Paul took a turn for the worse the other day and she needed to talk to the staff about the payments. There was no way she was going to be able to make the same amount now. Not until she found another job.

Instead of finding a way to lift a small burden from her shoulders, Danielle now had more. The hospital couldn't work with her anymore than what they'd already done, and her father was causing more problems. He wanted Paul looked at by a specialist...again...and moved to a private room. Both things cost too much, and her father gave the hospital staff a hard time for not doing what he wanted.

As usual, it always came down to what her father wanted, and what he thought Paul deserved. Always the best, but never worry about the cost.

Danielle was tired of this; tired of being the one to fix the family problems; tired of having to deal with it all. But mostly she was tired of how her father held her back from her own goals in life. She wanted out! Plain and simple.

"Ms. Hughes!"

Danielle stopped and tried to put on a smile as the lady she had just spoken with about the costs rushed up to her. Even listening seemed hard when she felt like the world was crashing down on her and she couldn't stop it.

"Ms. Hughes. I'm sorry, but Mr. Remington would like to speak with you tomorrow. He told me it's very urgent."

Danielle suppressed a groan. She knew how the Remington's were. Cold, heartless pricks. The only thing they ever cared about was money. Making it and taking it away from others. The only one that was somewhat decent was their son, Nate, but still he thought about appearances. She remembered him from school, always dating the prettiest girls, the ones that had money also. To Danielle, Nate was nothing but a spoiled brat with a golden spoon in his mouth.

"What time?" she asked on a sigh.

The lady gave her a sympathetic smile. "Three. He's flying in tonight for other business in the hospital."

"I bet he is," she said under her breath, "Fine. I'll be here."

Danielle walked to her brother's room. She didn't go in, but stood in the hall looking at him through the glass. Paul was getting worse and there wasn't anything she could do to help. All of her ideas and resources were tapped out, something she needed her father to understand.

* * * *

"No, you don't understand!" Danielle yelled at her father from the kitchen table. "We don't have that kind of money! He's fine in the room he's in."

Robert Hughes looked hard at his daughter. Danielle could see the barely banked fury raging in him, "You listen to me. That is your brother in there dying. I intend to make him as comfortable as possible until a new liver comes for him."

"You don't understand. If there is no money, there is no liver. I have been telling you this for months. You are spending what little we have."

"Something will come," Marie Hughes said in a soft voice, "Have faith."

"Have faith?" Danielle cried out in disbelief. "Mother, do you even know what he tried to do this time?"

"Don't you bring her into this!" Robert yelled.

"Don't bring her into this?" Danielle rubbed her hands over her face then into her hair. She tried to take a deep breath in order to get her temper under control. It didn't work. "She has just as much right to know what is going on as anyone in this house. I'm tired of working for nothing, while you take everything I earn. I am so tired of you dragging us down into the shit hole you love to wallow in." She looked at her mother with dampness in her eyes, "There is no more money. On top of that, my hours at work are getting cut. I can't pay for Paul's room any more."

"What did you do this time?" her father yelled, his face getting red.

"Nothing," she cried, looking at him as if he'd lost his mind, "But I will tell you one thing I'm going to do. I'm done supporting you. I'll work out something for the bills from now on for Paul, but after that I'm done!"

"That's your brother, girl," he told her in a deadly voice. "Where the fuck do you get off dictating to me what you will, or will not do?"

"I know that's my brother, and I also know that I have never had a life since he got sick. It's time for you to act like the man of this house, and not the grieving parent." Danielle stood up from the table. She looked at both of her parents, "It's time for you two to figure out how to deal with this. In the afternoon, I have to face Mr. Remington about the bills that have gone unpaid. When the back bills are fixed, I'm done!"

Danielle walked out of the kitchen with her father still raging at her Danielle slammed the door shut sitting down on her bed. It wasn't too long before her mother walked quietly into her room, sitting down on the bed next to her.

"You know these things will fix themselves," her mother said quietly, "They always do."

Danielle sighed, "This time they won't. I've been telling you both for the past few months that we needed to be careful with the money. We don't have enough to cover the cost of the room, let alone the equipment."

Marie patted her daughter on the knee. "I have faith. It will all work out."

* * * *

Danielle woke early expecting to go in and do her short shift at work, but the restaurant manager called and told her not to come in. The restaurant had failed another health inspection and was forced to close its doors. Everyone was out of a job now.

She walked out to the kitchen for breakfast, working hard at looking normal. Her father grunted his morning welcome and her mother smiled brightly. Breakfast was a quiet and somber time. Paul was the one that used to brighten the day. He would spend the morning telling them all the things he was doing at college. How his date with the latest cheerleader went or what kind of trouble he was having in one of his classes.

When Paul was around, Danielle didn't seem to exist. All of the family attention went straight to Paul. The only one in the family that did seem to give a damn about her was Paul, but to Danielle it wasn't the same thing. She wanted the love that their father gave to him.

The stingy part of her was so happy the day Paul got sick. She thought for the first time she would get some of that praise, some of that love. All she got was the burden of how they were going to fix Paul. The day they found out his liver was not doing the job and that he needed to be put on the list for a new one, was the day her life stopped. That day almost killed their father. Robert became a very bitter man. The hurtful words he said to Danielle crushed her last hope for a loving father-daughter relationship.

"That should be you in that bed dying. Not my boy!"

Her mother wasn't any better. Marie crawled inside herself and stayed there. She died in a way. The cheerful woman was no more than a shell. She went through the daily routine of life, but never lived again. The whole house became just a house, not a home.

"I have to go into work early," Robert grumbled behind his paper, "You need to go and see your brother."

"That will work. I have a meeting with Mr. Remington. I can stay with Paul until then," she replied, taking a sip of her juice.

"What about work?"

"There is no work."

Robert slammed his paper down on the table hard. "What the hell did you do now?"

"How come every time something goes wrong around here you think it's my fault?" she asked with gritted teeth.

"What happened?" he demanded, "We needed that job of yours."

"Yes, I know. My money was paying for Paul, while God only knows where your money is going." Danielle stood up from the table. She took her purse and jacket heading for the door. "It would be nice if for once in my life I could have a life."

She slammed the door shut before her father could make another crack at her. Danielle didn't know what she was dreading more, seeing Paul, or having to deal with Mr. Remington. Neither was appealing to her at this moment.

* * * *

Nathaniel Remington sat in the back of his father's Royals Royce reading over the files that the hospital sent. With the sudden death of his father in a plane crash, he was now the head of the family and in charge of all of the business affairs. He found out that after the death of his father he was also part of the board at the hospital and one of his responsibilities dealt with past due bills. That was his father's favorite thing in life. Money.

Nathaniel, or Nate to his friends and family, was six foot three and built like a football player. He had sandy brown hair that didn't quite reach his shoulders, and he always kept it brushed back from his eyes. His handsome face and his baby blues could always get him what ever and whom ever he wanted in his youth. Nate had been compared to a *Brad Pitt* look alike in college. Talking about his good looks was something that would always make him blush but they never failed to have all of the hottest girls in college wanting to go out with him.

He read over the files, noticing that the problems the hospital wanted him to deal with were over money and health issues. Four families that were facing life or death issues were very broke, and the hospital wanted Nathaniel to kick them out. The one thing that the society didn't know about Nathaniel was that he wasn't a cutthroat like his father. He didn't break things down into the harsh black and white. He looked harder at the root of the problem. Nathaniel wanted to know why someone was having financial trouble, from what he'd read in a file. After all, his grandfather always said there was more to a family than what was in a file.

He closed his second file on a sigh, rubbing his eyes as he dreaded having to read the other two. In the past few months, trying to fill his father shoes and deciding it was time to do things his way was taking its toll. He never knew how hard of a man his father was. How uncaring he became. Nathaniel recently learned how *much* of a bastard the man really was.

There was only one file he had yet to read and Nate decided to read that one in his office. In the past few weeks, he had managed to make big changes in the way the company was run and in who continued to work there. Most of the staff on the board of his family's company was just as cutthroat as his father had been. They loved to crush other family companies. Merging them with his own then selling the stock was the coldest kind of business anyone could do. For as long as he could remember his father telling him, Remington Acquisitions was the company that crushed others. It made the family so rich that it stopped bringing happiness. Now the money caused most of his family to think they were better than others. If there was a company out there in trouble of going under, Nate's father and grandfather were able to smell it out. They could take it over and bring that company down to its knees. The final killing point was when they sold the stock and never looked back.

His secretary handed him a small stack of messages. Most of them were from his new lawyer letting him know about a few of the petty suits his father's men were planning on filing against him. Nate even had one from his father's lawyer threatening to sue him. The message only made him laugh.

"Nancy," Nate said to his secretary as he tossed a few of the messages in the trash, "Any more calls from my father's lawyer I want you to hang up on him. I don't have time for this petty crap."

"Yes, Sir."

"And call the hospital. Have them call and change my appointment to ten and have it here. When that's done, let Thomas know about these messages from the former staff. That's what I pay him to take care of."

"Yes, Sir. Shall I go ahead and direct those calls to his office?"

Nate smiled at the elderly woman, "That's why I hired you. You can read my mind."

"I do my best," she smiled back.

Nate handed her two of the files in his hand. "Call these two families and see about working out some kind of payment plan. These two here I will take care of myself. In fact one of them is the appointment." Nate opened one file and frowned when he started to read it.

"Something wrong?" Nancy asked.

"Hughes. I know I have heard that name before," he mumbled to himself

Nancy stood up from her desk with another stack of files. She handed a binder to Nate and pushed him down the hall, "The board meeting that you requested is waiting for you. Your other meeting with Dunkin Industries is at ten sharp. After that you have your appointment with the family from the hospital, then another board meeting."

"Another fun filled day of the suits," Nate grumbled as he handed his file off to Nancy and took the binder from her.

"You have a lunch meeting with your lawyer, then another meeting across town with the company your father was working on before he died. After that your day is all yours."

They stopped at the door to the board room where Nate shut the binder he was reading to look at Nancy. "For what I pay you, one would think you could look like you're as busy as me."

Nancy straightened his tie for him before she handed him another folder. "For what you pay me I do just fine. Want me to do more, pay more."

Nate smiled. "Yep. You're the icing on my cake."

"Then go in there and bake up a winner."

* * * *

Danielle rode the public bus for almost an hour before she got off and transferred to another. She was slightly upset when she got the call from the hospital before she went to visit Paul. Remington, all of a sudden, decided he wanted to have this meeting in his office in the heart of the city, a trip that was going to cost her twenty in bus fare. Thank God her father was at work when the call came. Any time a call from the hospital or from Remington came, it had to be bad news.

She was ten minutes late by the time she got on the elevator heading up, ten minutes late and hungry as hell. Not a good way to start off a meeting with the one person that could save her and all of her problems at the hospital. If he wasn't willing to work with her then Danielle didn't know what she would do.

On the top floor, Danielle found that all she could really do was look around. She had never been to Remington Industries before and what she saw of it so far was very impressive.

"May I help you, Miss?"

Danielle turned and smiled as an older woman, no more than five-five, came walking up to her. She had salt and pepper hair that was curled and styled neatly. She wore a soft blue business suit with matching pumps.

"Yes, um, I'm here to see Mr. Remington," Danielle said.

"Ah, you must be his ten. Follow me. Mr. Remington is expecting you."

Danielle swallowed hard and followed the lady down the hall. Her hands started to shake as she thought about this meeting. Nothing good could come out of this. *He's going to give us the boot and then Paul is going to die. I just know it!*

The woman knocked on a set of double doors. She smiled at Danielle as she opened them. "Mr. Remington? Your ten o'clock is here."

"Thank you, Nancy."

Danielle walked into the large office and looked around. She jumped when the doors closed behind her. The office was the normal rich office that she'd seen in magazines. Built in bookshelves were lined with leather books. Leather furniture accented the room and in front of her, centered before a large window, was a stately cherry oak desk. As Danielle looked around, she decided the room seemed to be cleaned out. The boxes in the far corner proved what she thought.

"Please, have a seat."

Danielle looked at the man standing in a dark corner reading a file. Suddenly she felt as if she was a child being punished. She walked over to one of the leather chairs in front of the desk and awaited her fate.

"Okay," he said.

She watched as he walked back to his desk, but her heart suddenly gave a jump when she saw who it was that sat down.

"I've looked over your file and…" He looked up from his reading and she imagined his expression held just as much a surprise as hers. "Dannie?"

"Nathaniel? Nathaniel Remington? What are you doing here?" Danielle asked as shock ripped through her body, her voice trembling.

"This is my company," he explained. "My father died a few months ago."

"Oh, I'm sorry. I hadn't heard."

"Thank you." He smiled. "I thought I knew the name Hughes, but had no idea that it was you."

"Afraid so." Her voice dropped down and Nate gave her a quizzical look.

"I was expecting your father."

Danielle looked him straight in the eyes. Suddenly, she felt as if she was back in high school. "Afraid not. When it comes to the finances of my brother, it falls on my shoulders."

"I see." He frowned, not really understanding.

"I don't expect you to understand," she sighed. "Hell, even I don't."

"From what I've read, and from what you just told me, you have been taking care of your brother's needs since high school. Boy that is a lot on one's shoulders."

"Yes, it is."

Nate sat back in his chair and looked at her. It had been at least six years since he last saw Danielle. He was a few years older than her, but Nate could remember Danielle to this day in the history class that they shared. It was the one and only class he had with her, but something that first day hooked him. He never seemed to get her out of his head, even while dating other girls.

"Have you had lunch yet?" he asked suddenly.

Danielle gaped at him. "What?"

"Lunch. Have you had it yet?"

"No, but don't you think it's kind of early to have lunch?"

Nate smiled, "Okay. Brunch?" Danielle watched him as he picked up his phone, "Nancy? Please call Thomas and cancel our meeting."

"Yes, Sir. Shall I set it up for tomorrow?"

"That will be fine, Have the car brought around. Miss Hughes and I will be finishing this meeting over brunch."

Danielle looked at him as if he had lost his mind.

"Shall we?" he asked her with a bright smile on his face.

The only thing that Danielle could do was take his hand and let him lead her out of his office for a sudden brunch meeting.

Chapter Two

Nate took Danielle to the closest restaurant, *Landmark,* which just happened to be one of the best in the city. She'd seen it a few times when she was younger and ventured out without her father knowing about it. Having lived in Chicago all of her life Danielle found she wanted to see more of the city.

"I hope you don't think this is too fancy?" Nate asked as they sat down at their table.

Danielle looked around at the few guests, noticing right away that she was not dressed to their code, "I don't think I fit in here."

"Nonsense," he chuckled, "I think you fit perfect. These snobs need a little down to Earth company."

A waiter greeted them and handed her a menu and Danielle felt even more out of place. She knew that she didn't fit in here and couldn't for the life of her understand why he had brought her here for their meeting.

"Relax," he said as he read his own menu, "They won't bite."

"I really don't think I belong here." He looked over his menu and she went on, "I mean come on, Nate. I'm dressed in khaki slacks and they are in dresses and skirts."

Nate looked around the room and smiled at the ones that were still staring at them. He even waved at one table where two ladies were whispering. "Always did hate snobs. People like that are never happy."

"And you are?"

Nate put his menu down and leaned forward, "I wasn't raised with the golden spoon in my mouth, if that is what you are implying?"

"I wasn't implying anything," she told him softly, averting her eyes.

Nate grinned as he sat back in his chair, "Something tells me that I make you uncomfortable. Do I?"

"Yes and no." She met his eyes as a waiter walked up to their table.

Nate smiled. "Order what ever you like. Their steak here is great."

"Steak?"

"Why not?" His eyes sparkled when he looked at her. "Can't talk business on an empty stomach." When his only response was a frown, Nate took it upon himself to order for both of them. "Two steaks and eggs. Coffee, orange juice, and toast."

"And how would you like your steak, Miss?" the waiter asked.

Danielle kept her eyes on Nate as she spoke. She thought to herself, why not. Why not let him buy her a great meal before he tossed her brother out. "Well done, please."

"And you, Sir?"

Nate also kept his eyes on Danielle. "Medium well."

The moment the waiter walked away, Danielle started the meeting. "I know the hospital wants you to throw my brother out."

"Yes, they do."

"Is that what you're going to do then?"

Nate's eyes stayed on her as the waiter came back with two glasses of fresh orange juice and a pot of coffee. He poured them both a cup before leaving again. Nate took a sip of the hot brew, and she didn't touch a thing.

"Are you always this tense?" he asked her with his charming smile in place. "Relax, Dannie. I only brought you out to brunch so we can talk. I want to get to know you."

"Why?"

"Why not?"

Danielle sighed, "Nate, we come from very different worlds."

"True, but in a small way we're not that different." She settled back in her chair with a slump and crossed her arms over her chest. "Dannie, I wasn't raised with all of this. My mother made sure I was as down to earth as you are today."

"I find that hard to believe," she snorted.

16

"See," he charmed back, "There is much you don't know about me."

Danielle shook her head and sighed again. She was about to say something smart to him when the waiter came back with their food. She looked down at the plate and couldn't believe how much food was on it. A large, thick boneless loin steak with two large eggs over easy. Two slices of bread, toasted, were cut and arranged around the food and two bowls of fruit were also placed on the table.

"Will there be anything else?" the waiter asked.

"I think that will do it," Nate answered, placing his napkin on his lap. "So," he went on as he began to cut his steak, "You were about to say something?"

Danielle also placed her napkin on her lap but instead of digging into her food she looked at him with one elbow resting on the table. "I need to know what your plans are for the bill. I have to have something to tell my father."

Nate chewed on his food as he picked up the orange juice. He seemed to be thinking hard over his answer, carefully gauging how to handle this. "I know your family situation, Dannie. You're not the only family that the hospital wants me to kick out. The only difference with you is that I like you. It also helps that we went to school together."

Danielle laughed, "We only had one class together."

"Yes, and it was that one class that made a big impression on me." He cut off another piece of meat, popping it in his mouth before he sat back in his chair. "Let me tell you something about me that not too many others know. I was raised by my mother. She left my father when I was about two. They never divorced, mainly because he didn't believe in it. For the longest time the only thing I ever knew about my father was that he sent checks regularly." He took a drink of his juice, looking at her with a very serious expression on his face. "She raised me in about the same manner you were raised. She worked, we lived off of her paychecks and all the money my father sent paid for was the house we stayed in. She invested the rest into a college account."

"Cut to the chase, Nate," she sighed again. "I need to get back to Paul."

He wiped his mouth with his napkin before he sat back again. "I never knew I had money until I was thirteen. That was when I came to live with my father. I finished growing up watching him be a bastard to anyone that didn't have either the money he had or position. I'm not like him. Never wanted to and never plan to." When she opened her mouth to speak again, Nate held up his hand. "Hold that thought. I have an idea, and you can think on this. I have a social gathering at the end of the week. It's for this company I saved from ruin. I'd like for you to be my date."

"Your date?" She was confused by his request and knew it showed on her face and in her voice as she sat there and looked at him as if he had lost his mind.

"Yes. We can even call this a business deal if you like. In exchange for your company I'll take care of the past bills at the hospital."

"You want to pay me to go out with you?" At his nod she went on, "Won't that make me a paid escort or something?"

Nate couldn't help himself and laughed, "Escorts have sex. We'll be having dinner."

Danielle placed her napkin on the table and pushed herself away. "Thank you for the brunch, Nathaniel, but I think I am going to have to pass on the offer." She stood up and was about to grab her purse when he finally spoke.

"Sit down, Danielle." His voice was cold as he spoke. "Our meeting isn't over."

Danielle looked around, noticing how people at the other tables were looking over at her. She sat back down, but kept her eyes away from him.

"You don't have a job. Your family owes more money than they make to the hospital and any day a liver could come through for your brother. If that happens you won't get it because of what you owe. Am I close?" With her curt nod of agreement, Nate went on, "Then please tell me what the problem is with what I suggested?"

"We're from different worlds, Nate. I said that from the moment you brought me into this place. Little rich boy wants to go play around in the alley. I'm not a charity case or a fucking snow white that needs the knight in shining armor to come to the rescue. I have always been able to figure this shit out and I can do it again."

"This time it's different." His voice changed tones again. It was as cold as when he commanded her to sit. Now it was gentle with a hint of caring, "You're going to need some help this time. Whether you want it or not."

"So it has come to this?" she mumbled to herself.

"One date. That's all I ask. In return you get some much needed help." He offered her a charming smile. "And I will even toss in the dress."

"One date. Nothing more?" she asked cautiously.

"Maybe dinner, but it would be all platonic. I won't ask you to come and spend the night at my house if that's what you're implying."

After a lengthy pause, Danielle decided what she needed to do, "Alright. I'll go to this thing with you."

Nate smiled brightly, placing his napkin back in his lap, "Now that is all settled will you please eat your steak? It really is the best."

Danielle grinned as she also placed her napkin back in her lap. The moment she took her first bite of the meat, she closed her eyes and sighed.

"I told you so." Nate grinned. "Now, care to give me your size so I might have a dress and shoes sent over. This thing is at the end of the week."

* * * *

Danielle sat in her window seat in her bedroom looking out the window wondering how the hell she got herself into the mess she was in now. A date! Of all the things she could have gotten out of the lunch a date was not one of them. How the hell was she going to explain to her parents that she was going out on a date with Nate Remington? She could just imagine the things her father was going to say when it came out.

A knock on her bedroom door broke into Danielle's thoughts. She told who ever it was to come in. She was shocked to see that it was her mother.

"Is everything alright?" Marie asked in a tender voice, "I was wondering how the meeting went?"

Danielle stood up, brushing her fingers into her hair, "Fine," she told her mother with a dead voice, "Couldn't be better."

Marie sat down on the foot of the bed and patted a spot for Danielle to join her. When she did, Marie took her daughter's hand, "I haven't been much of a mother to you since Paul got sick."

"That isn't true," Danielle protested.

"Yes it is," Marie told her with a somewhat sterner voice. "I know I haven't. His sickness hit us so hard that I thought I was going to die. And when they told us that no one in our family was a match to help him, well I don't know what I was then," she sighed. "All I'm saying is that as much as you think your father doesn't love you, he does. Your father is just suffering in a way all his own. He shouldn't have put the burden of this on your shoulders."

Danielle pulled her hand away from her mother's and stood up with a deep sigh, "Well he did, and now I'm cleaning up his mess. I worked out a deal with Mr. Remington to take care of the back bills. I think when that is taken care of Dad should be able to handle the rest."

Marie nodded her head and stood up as well. "I understand. Why don't you go freshen up then and come help me with dinner? Your father will be home soon and knowing the past bills are going to be taken care of should help put him in a good mood."

Danielle watched her mother leave the room, closing the door softly behind her. She mumbled to herself, "I doubt it."

Dinner was a simple event, but one full of tension. Danielle found that she only picked at her food as she thought about Nate and the upcoming date. Her father kept glaring at her and her mother hung her head in complete silence.

"Those sons of bitches!" Robert suddenly yelled, tossing his fork to the side and slamming his fist down on the table, "All the fucking years I gave them bastards and this is how they repay me!"

"What happened?" Marie asked her husband in a soft voice.

"The plant is closing down by the end of the month. Bankrupt," he snarled, "Can you believe it? They're not even going to give us our profit sharing. Said we're damn lucky to be able to draw unemployment from them."

"Oh no!" Marie cried out, her eyes suddenly filling up with tears.

Danielle knew what was about to come before it was even said. She braced herself as he looked at her with the cold eyes that she was so used to.

"You're going to have to get off that ass of yours and find a job," Robert snapped, "I wont have you lounging around the house eating my food while your mother and me bust our asses."

Danielle opened her mouth when the doorbell rang. Instead of getting into a word fight with her father like she did every night, she placed her napkin on the table and got up. When Danielle opened the door, she was speechless. Two different delivery men stood on her steps with packages in their hands.

"Ms. Hughes?" one asked.

"We both have a delivery for you from Mr. Remington. Can you please sign here?"

Danielle thought she was in a dream as the men handed her four large shopping bags with *Von Maur* on the side. It was one of the best stores in the city to shop, if you had money that is. One of the bags had a large box sticking out of it.

"What the hell is that?" Robert barked from behind her, "Did you go down town to spend some damn money! Money that we don't have!" he screamed.

"I didn't buy anything!" Danielle screamed back, shutting the door, "Nate Remington sent this stuff over."

"And why would he do that?" Robert demanded in a some what calmer voice.

"Because I have to go to a dinner meeting with him on Friday." She gave him a cold look as she walked past him to her room, "Its how I am paying back the past bills."

"What!" he yelled again.

Danielle stopped and turned around, "He needed a date for a board thing on Friday. Asked if I would join him and in return, he would help take care of the past bills. The bills the hospital wants to use to toss us out on the street." She took a deep breath before she went on, "So if you want to throw your names at me then go ahead. I did what I could to get us somewhat ahead."

"Ahead?" he snarled again, "You call whoring yourself out getting us ahead?"

"I'm not sleeping with the man!" she shouted, feeling her own anger rise,

"I'm joining him at a dinner where there will be lots of other people. If you can't handle that, then that's your problem."

Danielle rushed to her room and slammed the door shut, locking it. She closed her eyes and leaned against the door as her father started bellowing down the hall. She couldn't help but hear every nasty name he called her.

After a few moments, she tossed the bags on the bed and went to turn her stereo on to block out her father's raging. She was just about to hit the power button when she heard a faint ringing coming from one of the bags. With a frown on her face, Danielle walked over to her bed and started to look in the bags, following the sound. She was very surprised to find a small cell phone resting in a simple, small purse.

"Hello?" she answered it cautiously.

"Ah, good, you got the bags!"

Danielle smiled as she sat down on the bed. "You sent over a cell phone?"

"Well I thought this way we can stay in touch and you can keep in contact with your brother. And don't worry about the bill. It's all covered," Nate told her.

Danielle's smile widened "You really are going over board here. We're only going out on one date and you're making it feel like I am spending a week with you."

22

Nate laughed over the phone, "Now there's an idea."

"I'm serious!"

"So am I!" His voice dropped in tone, "The things I could show you."

"What is all this stuff anyway?" She changed the subject quickly, shaking her head as she heard him laughing again.

"*It*'s everything you're going to need for Friday. A dress, shoes, stockings, the works. And I don't want to hear anything about paying me back either. We made a deal and I'm upholding my part."

"This is too much."

"If you think this is too much then girl you should see what I could do for you in a week."

Danielle felt chills go down her spine at his words. In her wildest dreams she couldn't imagine what he could do if given the time. "So what time on Friday?"

"I'll be there to personally pick you up at five. The dinner party is at six, but it takes a little over an hour to get there."

"Then why not pick me up earlier?"

"Because, my dear…" Chills went down her spine again the way his voice dropped down with the 'my dear', "No one is ever on time to these things and I don't plan on being the first one there either. I might even have the driver take the long way."

Danielle thought for a few seconds before she spoke, "Can you make it at four. I would rather not leave the house when my father is home."

"Yeah…we can do that. I guess I could show you some of the finer points to downtown."

"Don't you mean the rich side of the neighborhood?"

Nate chuckled, "I never said that."

"You didn't have to."

Nate sighed into the phone, "Listen Dannie. Stop trying to make me see you in a light that I don't. When I look at you, I see the richest person alive. You're not a snob who expects. You are a down to earth girl that enjoys the simple things. When we had lunch today, I felt just like I did when my mother was alive. I felt down to earth. I like that feeling and for the strangest reason

I like feeling that way with you. If I'm moving fast than I am sorry. But even without the money I have now, if I saw something I wanted I went right for it." There was a long pause before Nate went on again, "It is getting late, and I have an important meeting in the morning. I'll swing by to pick you up after work."

"That will work. I'll be ready."

"Great! I'm looking forward to seeing you on Friday."

"Night, Nate."

"Night, Dannie."

Danielle hung the phone up and groaned into her hands, "What the hell have I gotten myself into?"

Chapter Three

Friday morning Danielle made sure she was the first one up. She showered, dressed, and was out the door in record time. Her first stop was to the bank. As much as she hated to have to do it, Danielle withdrew most of her savings. If she was going to go out and rub elbows with the rich then she needed to at least look like she might belong.

Picking up a sandwich along the way, Danielle headed for the beauty salon. She ended up spending the whole day there getting the works. Her hair was washed, trimmed, and then fixed on top of her head in the latest fashion. She then had her eyebrows waxed, along with her legs and along her bikini line. Nails were done and painted a soft pink along with her toes, after a full pedicure. Another big splurge was buying herself a new complete set of make-up. She even sat and had the lady show her how to use everything and which shades would be the best. By the time she was finished it was close to three. Danielle had less than an hour to get home and get dressed before Nate would pick her up.

Back in her room, Danielle dug into the boxes that were in the bags. New stockings, black, with a matching garter belt, bra, and panties were in one box. Black shoes were in another box that had at lcast three-inch heels. They were simple slip on shoes that had a velvet feel to them on the outside.

As she sat on the bed in the new under garments, pulling the stockings up her legs and clipping them to the garter belt, Danielle got her real first taste of what money truly felt like.

The last box for her to open contained the dress. She was so shocked when she pulled the lid off that her hands shook and she was almost afraid to touch it. A designer dress lay on cream-colored tissue. It was a short dress with thin straps and looked to be made of the finest silk.

It was the softest thing she'd ever touched in her life. Danielle picked it up by the straps and held it out at arms length to look at it. Even though it was simple and black it was still gorgeous. Because of the back being cut so low, Danielle had to take the bra off in order to wear it.

She walked to her mirror behind her door and watched herself as she stood in her panties, stockings with garter belt, and heels. She watched as she stepped into the dress, slowly putting the straps into place on her shoulders. Twisting around, she looked at the back side. Her whole back was exposed and it reached down to the waist line of the dress.

Looking at herself, Danielle felt like a princess in some kind of fairy tale. Her hands brushed over the dress and her nipples hardened at the feel of the silk over them. Danielle had to admit that she did feel very sexy in the short thing. She only wondered if Nate would think the same thing.

As the time drew nearer to four, Danielle quickly put a few pieces of make-up in the small bag that matched her dress. She also picked up the thin wrap that matched and walked out of her room to the front door. The same moment her hand touched the knob someone knocked on the door.

Nate stood at the door and with the first look he got of Danielle his jaw dropped, "Wow!"

Danielle blushed and looked down at her shoes, "Then I guess I don't have to ask if it meets with your approval."

"I'm speechless," he said in wonder, "Turn around."

Danielle held out her arms and turned around so he could see the whole thing. "Well?"

"I must say you are a vision," he breathed out, taking her hand in his own, "Completely breath-taking."

Danielle felt her insides melt as he brought her hand up to his lips. Before he kissed it he turned it over and kissed her wrist. Danielle thought her legs were going to give out then when he looked up at her as his lips stayed within inches of her skin.

She had to clear her throat in order to speak. "Shouldn't we get going?"

Nate smiled, "Yes. We need to stop off at my house so I can change." He motioned with his hand for her to head to the car. "You don't mind, do you?"

"No." She smiled back in a nervous manner. "If I'm dressed like this then there is no way you can go dressed in your business suit."

Nate motioned for his driver to stay in the car. He reached to open the door but she beat him to it. "That we can't have."

Danielle blushed again as she slipped into the car. She giggled to herself as she watched him dash around the car to the other side. Her first thought was that he behaved like a high school boy out on his first date.

The drive to his city home took about thirty minutes. During the drive, Danielle kept catching Nate looking at her. At first, it made her very uncomfortable, but after joking about it, she now found it very empowering. She never thought of herself as a woman who could stop a man in his tracks. Nate was making her wonder about that now.

When they pulled up to his home she was shocked to find that he lived in a simple, yet important neighborhood. The first thought that came to her mind as she stepped out of the car was that she was going into the house of Thomas Crown from the movie, *The Thomas Crown affair*.

"I bought this place when I was eighteen and never told my father. Just fell in love with it one day on a drive. Worked at remodeling it slowly for years. By the time my father did find out I had the house for at least three years."

"It's beautiful," she told him in wonder as she followed him inside.

"I live on the first floor. The second has my office and a few guest rooms. I keep only two people on staff. One is a maid who comes in twice a week; the other is a gentleman who takes care of the rest. He is one hell of a cook," he chuckled. "I also have the library upstairs. Feel free to take a look around." He added, "I'm going to take a quick shower."

Danielle only nodded her head, as she looked around at all the different paintings on the wall. One in particular caught her attention. It was a large painting of a woman that looked very down to earth. When Danielle walked closer to it, she found that it was Nate's mother. Bridget Remington was engraved on a gold plate at the bottom.

Somehow, Danielle found herself in Nate's bedroom. She touched a pillow that she thought might be the one used when he was sleeping. Slowly she ran her hand down the side of the made bed and round to the other side. She was so surprised that everything in the room was so neat. Even for a man that had someone picking up after him, she had expected to find he had a tendency to leave things on the floor. The one thing that she did spot was his suit jacket draped over a chair.

On silent feet, she walked over to the jacket and picked it up. Closing her eyes, she took a deep breath, taking in Nate's scent deep into her lungs.

Danielle's eyes snapped open the second she heard the spraying of the shower. She turned to see steam coming out of a door that was halfway closed. What ever possessed her to walk to that door, she didn't know.

Blocking her body with the wall Danielle peeked into the bathroom and saw a sight that was sure to give her the hottest dreams for the rest of her life.

With his back to her, Nate stood in all of his naked glory. His arms were over his head, his head hanging down as double sprays of water beat down on him, one from the left, and another from his right. She licked her lips as he flexed his shoulder blades and her eyes traveled down his back to the tight cheeks of his ass. Danielle found that she was digging her hand into the wall just thinking about gripping that flesh.

She had seen movies and even seen a few boys naked in high school by accident, but never had she seen a man quite like this before. He was all muscle. Not one ounce of flab marred his perfect body.

Again, his ass and back flexed as he groaned. Danielle figured he was working out some tight muscles in his body and a part of her sooo wanted to be the one to work them out for him.

Her whole body tingled as she watched him move his neck back and forth. Thought of how his hands would feel on her body as she watched him rub the back of his neck crossed her mind.

Only when the steam from the shower threatened to ruin her make-up did Danielle back away from the door and leave the room. Never once did she know or suspect that Nate knew she was there. That he caught sight of her in the bathroom mirror and made an extra show by flexing his body for her.

In fact Nate found it very exciting to have her standing there watching him shower. The only problem that he had now was that his body was rock hard with need. Need for her to join him.

It was five-thirty by the time he came out of his room dressed. He would have been out sooner, but found that his 'problem' would not go away on its own. Nate also found that just looking at her again in that dress was starting the need within him all over again

He stood in the doorway of the kitchen just watching her as she was leaning over the bar reading a magazine that had been laying there. Thoughts of coming up close behind her and touching her back over powered him.

Nate ended up clearing his throat, which got her attention, "Ready to go?"

Danielle smiled at him, "Guess about as ready as I'm going to get."

He offered her his arm as he picked up his dress coat and her wrap. "Oh I wouldn't worry too much. The only one that might bite tonight is me."

Danielle laughed, "Is that a fact?"

He opened the door for her, and then leaned in real close, "I could make it a promise," he whispered in her ear.

Danielle took her wrap from him and blushed as she walked out into the night and to the waiting car.

* * * *

The dinner party that Nate took Danielle to was a cold event to her. Tables were set around the place and everyone was assigned a seat. The only reason Nate was invited to the place was because he saved the company from going under.

Something he told Danielle that his father loved to do was steal them then sell them. That was his father's way.

Nate was very polite when he introduced her to the guests. They were very shocked to know that they went to school together and were still friends. Danielle could tell right off that the women at the party wanted Nate and didn't like the fact that he had brought her. For most of the dinner and through the speeches, Danielle sat there quietly. When the host announced that there was a special treat of dancing, Danielle took that as a moment for escape. She found a nice quiet spot on a balcony and leaned against the railing in peace.

"I've been looking for you."

Danielle smiled when she heard Nate's voice, "I needed to get away from the looks and the noise."

"Ah, the women are showing their teeth again," he joked, coming up to stand next to her.

"Something like that." Danielle worked hard at not smiling. She saw Nate from the corner of her eye watching her, "Ended up being a very nice night out."

"You can say that again," he agreed softly.

Danielle looked at him and her heart started to pound in her chest. Nate's expression was intense and full of emotion. She found that she didn't know if she could say anything. And if she did speak, would the words make any sense?

Her mouth suddenly went dry as his head slowly lowered. She watched as his lips got closer and closer to her own. However, just before his touched hers Danielle sucked in her breath, closed her eyes, and pushed away from him.

"I can't," she told him as she breathed out in a rush with her eyes still closed, "I'm sorry."

"Don't apologize," he said softly, 'I'm the one to blame here." He smiled, "Guess I can't help myself tonight."

"Don't blame yourself," she groaned and turned back around to look at the city. "Guess I just have a lot on my mind again."

"Well I was hoping that one thing would have been taken care of. Is there anything else I can do?"

"I don't think there's anything anyone can do at this point."

"Try me."

Danielle took a deep breath before she turned and looked back at Nate. "It's my father. The factory he works for is shutting the doors at the end of the month. He's going to be out of a job, and with my mother being on medical leave from her breakdown I don't see us getting out of the hole he put us in."

"I guess in a strange way I didn't see how much of the family troubles your father really does put on your shoulders."

"I'm sorry, Nate. I shouldn't bring something like this up. At least not here." She pinched the bridge between her nose as tension started to build in her. "What you have done for us has helped more than you know."

"But it isn't enough?" He cocked his head to the side. "Is it?" Danielle tried to look away but Nate took hold of her chin and forced her to look at him, "Is it?"

"No," she breathed out as a set of helpless tears threatened to fall.

Nate nodded his head and kissed her suddenly on the forehead, "Come on. Let's leave."

"But what about your party?" she asked as he dragged her by the hand.

"What about it?" He looked over his shoulder at her. "We made a presence."

Instead of taking her home, as Danielle expected, Nate would take her back to his place. He walked her up stairs to the library where he poured her a glass of scotch.

"I don't know if you've felt what I have, Dannie, but there is something between us." He looked at her as he took his dinner jacket off, tossing it to a chair. "I like you and I hate seeing you with this much of a burden on your shoulders."

"Get to the point," she said and crossed her arms over her chest, waiting.

Nate bit his lower lip as he thought about the right words he was going to need. He knew what he wanted but wasn't sure as to how to tell her.

"I like being with you, Dannie. I don't have to put up a front with you like I do with other people. I can be myself. Completely." When she only frowned at him, Nate went on, "I have the money to make all of your problems, and troubles simply go away."

"At what price?" Danielle asked in a shaky voice.

"At the price of your companionship," he told her frankly.

"Let me see if I get this right." She walked to the other side of the room, sitting her glass on one of the tables. "You want to pay me to be your *companion* for how long? And what might that include?"

"Well now that would depend on the money." When she turned around and looked at him he gave her a sexy smile, "Now wouldn't it?" She opened her mouth to speak but Nate held his hand up to her. "Don't answer me now. Go home and sleep on the idea. In the morning, come by my office and we can talk about it further. Include the what of the deal."

Danielle nodded her head in agreement and headed for the door. When she opened it she turned to find Nate right behind her. "Can I please have your driver take me home alone? I really would like to think about what you just said."

"Absolutely. I will make sure Nancy changes my morning schedule and expect to you see in the morning."

* * * *

At nine in the morning, Danielle stood outside Nate's office building pacing the sidewalk and twisting her hands. She was so nervous that she knew she was going to be either sick or piss her pants. She kept telling herself that going out on a few dates wouldn't be that bad. She could dress up and play pretend. Have some great food; a few new dresses and that would be it. But something else was screaming at her. One word, as a matter of fact. *Mistress*!

She was completely stupid. Danielle knew that Nate wanted her to be his weekend fling, she just needed to decide if that was the only way out or not. And another problem crept into her mind. One that could really cause a lot of trouble. Danielle really wanted to.

When she looked at her watch again, she noticed only two minutes had passed since the last time she checked. Danielle thought that it was about time she went up and got this whole thing over with.

Again, it took her almost ten minutes of talking herself into getting on the elevator. She kept pacing back and forth in front of it as her hands shook. The security guard kept his eyes on Danielle and she thought to herself that he must think she was going up to rob someone.

"Shit, shit, shit!" she mumbled to herself, "Can I do this?"

"Ma'am? Are you alright?" the guard asked her.

"Yes, just great!"

He gave her a kind smile. "If you're the one Mr. Remington is waiting for, I might let you know he's waiting. He's called down here at least three times checking on you."

"I bet he has," she grumbled.

"Well I'm sure you're making too much of this meeting." He walked over to the elevator, pressing the up button, "Might as well treat it like a band aid. Pull and get it over with quickly."

Danielle tried to give him a kind smile but failed. She was too nervous and if it wasn't for him almost pushing her she wouldn't be on the damn thing heading up to Nate. Danielle was so shocked when Nate's secretary was at the elevator to greet her.

"Ms. Hughes," the knowing tug on the woman's lips had her feeling like she was a peace of meat. "I was starting to wonder if you were going to come up at all. Mr. Remington is waiting for you in his office."

Danielle swallowed hard and pulled her shoulders back. She followed the woman down the hall to the double doors that led into the office and to Nate.

"Please, go right on in."

Danielle's hands shook so bad that she found opening the door was almost impossible. Even her throat felt dry and restricted. The only thing that seemed to push her into opening the door was the words from her father this morning.

"You had better help around here more young lady or your ass is out of this house!" Robert snarled.

"Help out?" Danielle questioned him with a look of disbelief on her face. "I think if anything I carry this household on my shoulders."

"Oh, you do, do you?" he smarted back in a high pitched voice, "You go out with some guy in a fancy dress and now you act all better than us." His voice dropped back down to his hateful self. "All you have done lately is drag your ass while your mother and I pick up the slack. You don't even go and visit your brother!"

Danielle shook her head to clear what had happened last night from her mind. She was so shocked to find her father waiting up for her; the fight that followed the moment the door closed wasn't a surprise.

"Well, dad," she said to herself again, "You made this bed, let's see if you can sleep in it after I am done."

Danielle opened then closed the door. She held her head high as she walked up to Nate. He rose from where he sat behind his desk and looked at her with the same intent expression on his face as she wore. Danielle walked up to the chair and took a seat. Looking at him square in the eye, she said, "Okay, Mr. Remington. Let's talk business."

Chapter Four

"Let's cut to the chase here, Dannie," Nate said. He walked around his desk to her chair. Gripping the arm rests he leaned near and lowered his voice so she wouldn't miss a single word. "For one whole week of your company I'll pay all of the outstanding medical costs for your brother. For you to stay with me for one week, I'll not only give you this very nice check, but I'll take care of his medical needs for the rest of his life."

Danielle swallowed hard as she looked up at Nate. Her heart pounded at his words and her body started to tingle at the thought of being close to him. After all this time and after she finally got rid of the hidden crush she had for him, now she had her chance. Now she could finally experience what all of the high school girls would talk about in gym class. Danielle remembered all too well the stories about how good he was in bed. How a special look from his baby blue eyes would have you melting at the knees. She was starting to think it was the look that he gave her now.

"So what's your answer?" he asked her calmly, moving away to sit on the edge of his desk.

Danielle stood up, turning her back on him and taking a few steps away. She felt so overwhelmed that she didn't really know what to do. What would he think or say when he found out she'd never been with a man before? That she never even got to date. Hell, she barely got to experience kissing thanks to her father.

"You want me to stay with you for one week? And you'll not only take care of my brother's medical needs but pay me one million dollars?" she turned and looked at him then, "What will that make me?"

"If you think it will make you a whore than think again." He looked at her with a straight forward expression. "We both win here, not just me or you."

"But, but you will expect me to sleep with you?" she stuttered.

"I will expect for you to be an honest companion. We will go to some dinners, plays, what ever your heart desires. And yes," he cocked his head to one side, and lowering his voice, "I want to sleep with you."

"Why?" her simple question seemed to take him aback.

"Excuse me?"

"Why me?" She pushed her hands into her jean pockets and looked at him from across the room. "Of all the girls you've had and can have, why me? Why not call up one of your old flings for the weekend?"

Nate crossed one leg over the other as he looked at her. He worked hard at not letting her see how badly he wanted her. "Maybe you're the one that makes me feel like there's more to me than money. Maybe you're the one with who I can truly be myself."

"Or maybe I'm the one that you never got back in school?" she challenged back.

"I won't sit here and lie to you, Dannie." He stood up, putting his own hands in his slack pockets, "I did want you back in high school. Even used to think about how to get you to go out with me. Take pride in the knowledge that you were the one girl back then that made me so nervous I couldn't breathe." He walked back around the desk taking his seat and picking up a file. "I will also let you know that I've done my homework. I know that your whole family is broke. Your father leans on you too much. I also bet that he has kept you under lock and key most of your life." He took a deep breath, leaned forward and rested his chin on a fist. "Members on the board want me to kick your family out and, if my father were still alive, that's just what would happen." He looked up at her again with a mixture of kindness and business on his face. "Is the thought of spending a week with me that bad?"

Danielle bit her lower lip as she looked around the office, thinking. She knew deep down that spending a whole week with Nate was all she dreamed about. To be in his arms and having him be her first was all she ever fantasized about. She also knew that her father would brand her a whore when he found out, but then again he was doing that now. The only way he wouldn't is if she had enough money to finally be on her own.

And that's when it hit her.

"Three million, along with taking care of my brother, then you have your week," she told him as her body shook with nerves.

Nate grinned and leaned back in his chair. He clasped his hands over his chest as he looked at her. "That's a lot of money for only one week."

"True." She felt her face heat up while she looked around the room again, avoiding his eyes. "I'm losing something more than my father's respect."

It took Nate the longest time for him to figure out what she was talking about and when it did the knowledge hit him hard. It slammed into him with such force that his cock sprang to life in an instant.

He couldn't believe his luck. She'd been a knock out in high school—still was. Nate couldn't believe that she was a virgin. Not by any means.

"Are you trying to tell me…" he asked but got cut off by her.

"Yes!" she gritted out at him, keeping her eyes averted from his.

Nate rubbed his chin then mouth, thinking, before he stood back up. Again he walked around his desk, but this time he walked up to her. "This changes things somewhat."

"Maybe this was a bad idea," she sighed out, finally looking up at him. "I'm sure I can figure something out for the money I need."

"Oh, this isn't a mistake," he told her softly. "In fact I'll pay the money and all expenses needed, but I want at least two weeks with you."

"WH…what?" she asked with barely any voice.

"You heard me." He smiled mischievously. "I want at least two weeks, with the possibility of more time with you." With her suddenly speechless, Nate when on, "Do we have a deal?"

Danielle finally nodded her head yes after a lengthy pause. "What am I supposed to tell my family?"

"First let me take care of your brother. I should have it all straightened out in no more than forty-eight hours. By tonight I'll have our personal contract sent to you along with the money."

She watched him write down a few things on a pad he had in his jacket.

"These are numbers that you'll need. One is my cell, the other a bank where the money will be transferred. Call the bank in the morning with instructions on how you want to handle the funds. I should have everything with the hospital finished by this evening, so I'll be around to pick you up after ten tonight."

"This is all going so fast," Danielle said to herself as she looked at the numbers on the paper he handed her.

"I'll be frank with you, Dannie. I've waited so long that to me this isn't going nearly fast enough." He smiled in his old high school charming way.

Danielle nodded her head again, but this time she felt stunned and in a haze. She just sold herself to her high school crush. How was one supposed to feel about that? A question she couldn't answer.

She walked to the door in the same haze but stopped when her hand touched the knob. She turned back around with a frown on her face and eyes to the floor. "Should we shake hands or something?"

Nate smiled, walking up to her. He took both of his hands and cupped her face, forcing her to look him in the eyes. "I have a better idea."

Now Danielle knew she was in a dream! His lips came down to her own with a kiss that swept her right off her feet.

It was a confusing kiss. At first it was demanding then changed to soft, then again to a gentle probing with his tongue. Danielle became lost and opened up her mouth to him. She moaned softly the moment his tongue touched her own and brought her arms up around his neck. Fingers raked into his soft hair while his own arms wrapped around her body. He pulled her as close to him as he could get, then took a few steps to the door where he pressed her against it.

"Mr. Remington?" the secretary buzzed on the intercom suddenly. It was enough to stop them cold in their tracks.

Danielle pushed at his chest to break the kiss, not an easy task to do. It seemed that neither wanted to end it.

With his eyes still closed, Nate planted his hands on the door above her head. His forehead still touched hers as he worked to control his breathing and raging body.

"Mr. Remington?" his secretary called again.

"I…um, I should leave," Danielle finally said.

"And I should let you go," he said as he opened his eyes and smiled down at her, "But find that I don't want to."

Danielle blushed again and pushed at his chest. This time Nate moved away. "I really need to go. I've a lot of stuff to do if you are expecting to pick me up later tonight."

Nate tried to straighten his suit and brush his hair with his hands. He cleared his throat and picked up the paper she dropped. Handing it back, he said, "Pack light. Everything you're going to need I'll take care of."

Danielle quickly left the office before anything else took place. Her hands shook and her mind spun as what she'd just done went through her mind. Not only did she save her brother's life and family, she sold herself. The funny thing was that Danielle didn't really feel any guilt over it. She had always wanted Nathaniel Remington. Always had a crush on him and compared all other boys to him. From what she heard, to spend a night with him was a treat that only the girls in his own class got to experience. And most of them were only a one night stand. She was going to spend two whole weeks in his company.

Walking to the bus stop Danielle smiled. She thought, *Hell, I would have slept with him back in high school for free if he only gave me the time of day.*

Nathaniel watched from his office window as the one girl of his dreams headed for the bus stop. His body was still on fire and his lips still tingled from the kiss. Nate had to admit to himself that he had it bad for Dannie Hughes. Always had and always would. Now he just needed to come up with a solid plan to keep her. Now that his father wasn't around to tell him what he could and couldn't do, he was free to pursue the one girl that he had loved since the moment he first laid eyes on her.

"Mr. Remington?"

Nate walked back to his desk the moment Dannie stepped onto the bus. "Well that shit is going to have to stop," he said under his breath to himself, "Yes, Nancy?"

"Your lawyer is here to see you. He said that you're expecting him, but there isn't anything written down."

"Yes, I'm expecting him," Nate told her, "Have him come in."

* * * *

Danielle sat on the crowded bus looking out the window thinking about all that happened in the past few days. First, the major money problem, then the hospital about to refuse treatment, her father about to lose his job, and now Nathaniel Remington coming to her rescue. If her lips weren't still tingling from that kiss she would think this was some kind of cruel dream.

The funny thing was, her memories of Nate dating in school never seemed to involve girls like her. There were fancy blondes that used to think their shit didn't stink, and the red heads that made a point of telling everyone how much better they were than anyone else. Danielle did remember being in a history class with Nate. She wondered if Nate remembered that they also shared the same gym hour.

To this day she could still see him with his shirt off playing a heated game of basketball with the guys. She could even hear the whispers and giggles from the other girls as they all watched the boys. Danielle recalled her last day in that gym class. Tracy Sullivan was his girlfriend at the time. A blonde with a big mouth to match her big breasts. She caught Danielle watching Nate and out of the blue started a fight with her. Instead of Danielle backing down to the girls like she always did, she fought back. Fought back and got suspended for three days for it. Paul thought it was funny, but her father didn't. He skinned her backside good, and then put her to work for the three days. By the time she got back to school everyone knew, and Tracy made a point to suck up all of the sympathy she could.

To keep peace, Danielle was transferred out of that gym class and put in another at a different time. It took care of one problem, but seemed to increase another. She could no longer watch Nate like she used to and had to work even extra hard at *not* making any kind of eye contact with him in history class. She had no idea that he was watching her, however. If she had known he was, she couldn't help wondering how things might have turned out differently.

At her stop, Danielle decided to purchase a special cup of coffee at *Starbucks*. As she sat at one of the outside tables drinking her coffee, her mind went back over the fight she had with her father and the deal she made with Nate. She knew her father didn't have much love for her, Danielle just didn't know it was this bad. At times she did wish it was her in that bed instead of Paul, but knew if it was the family wouldn't be fighting this hard to save her.

Guilt should be washing over her, but it wasn't. She knew that taking money from him was wrong, but what was she supposed to do? Her father put the whole family in a position that there was no getting out of. If she didn't take over and do this, then Paul would die. It would only be another thing Robert Hughes blamed his daughter for.

So as Danielle sat drinking her coffee she thought. Could she live with having her father calling her a whore? Or could she live with him blaming her when Paul died from the lack of medical attention he needed?

"That money could also get me out of there," she said to herself, "Out and away from him."

Standing up and tossing her cup in the trash, Danielle started the walk home with her mind made up. She could live with the disrespect from her father. She never had that much of it to begin with. What she couldn't live with was the knowledge that she had the power to save Paul and didn't.

"Besides," she told herself, "its only sex. People do it all the time. Why shouldn't I get to see what all the talk is about?" She walked up to the steps to her home and groaned. *Because, you dummy, this is your virginity you're selling. Once it's gone it isn't coming back,* Danielle chastised herself.

Danielle said a silent thank you that the house was empty when she walked in. She headed right to her room where she packed all of her bathroom needs, including her birth control. She looked at the small compact device and smiled. Originally she got this to help her out at that time of month. She silently hoped that she would also be able to use it for what it was intended, but never was given the opportunity. Danielle also made damn sure that her father never found it. Hell, even her mother didn't know how long she had been using contraceptives.

All the new things that Nate sent over went into the over night bag and the phone into her purse. She planned on stopping off to check in on Paul, before she met up with Nate; what she didn't plan on was her father being in the living room when she went down stairs.

"Dad!" Danielle cried in surprise, "What are you doing home so early?"

"Shift got cut short," he grunted behind his paper. "Thought I would get a start on looking for a new job. How is your job hunting going?"

Danielle's throat suddenly went dry. She dropped her bag behind the sofa, hoping that he wouldn't see it. "Well, um, something has come up so I won't be able to until later on."

Robert snapped his paper shut and came to his feet. "I don't want to hear any of your bullshit," he snapped at her, "We need all the income that we can get."

"I know that," she replied with a tight voice.

"Oh, you do, do you?" he sang with a snarl on his face. He walked up to her but stopped short when he saw the small bag on the floor. "And just where the hell do you think you're going?"

Danielle took a deep breath and braced herself for his anger. "I have to go on a…um…business trip."

Robert narrowed his eyes at his daughter. "With Remington?"

Steeling herself she gave a tight, "Yes."

Out of no where Robert smacked Danielle across the face, "You're turning out to be nothing but a slut!"

Danielle's hand went up to her burning cheek while tears came to her eyes. She couldn't believe that her father slapped her. He hadn't laid a hand on her in so long that this was a shock.

"I won't have you selling yourself to him and living in my house!" he barked at her.

Danielle didn't say a word to him or look at him. She picked up her bag with her hand still on her burning cheek. With tears falling down her face she walked out the front door.

Once she was a block away she stopped and sat on the steps of a neighbor's home, buried her face in her arms and cried. She couldn't tell if she was crying from the slap her father gave her or from the stress that just kept building up inside her.

As soon as the sobs stopped, but the tears didn't, Danielle dug into her purse until she found the cell phone that Nate had given her. With shaking hands she dialed his number, not sure what she was going to tell him.

"Hey!" Nate answered in a cheerful voice, "Couldn't wait to hear my voice again?"

"I had a fight with my father." She worked so hard to keep her voice level but failed. Another set of tears started, causing her voice to shake as she cried on the phone, "Can you come and get me now instead of tonight?"

"Where are you?"

Danielle couldn't hold back any longer. She broke down completely on the phone, "I'm…" she sobbed, "I'm a block from my house." She wiped at her face with a tissue, as people started to stare at her. "Sitting on one of my neighbor's steps."

"Stay right there. I'm leaving right now to come and get you."

Danielle hung the phone up and cried a new batch of tears. By the time Nate pulled up along the curb and jumped out of the car her eyes were red and swollen. He rushed up to her, kneeling down in front of her and taking her chin in his hand.

"Dannie?" he asked softly.

Danielle looked him in the eyes, knowing that she was a mess. "He hit me," she laughed through the tears, "He hit me, thinking I was out whoring around."

Nate brushed her hair away from her face to look at the red mark on her cheek. "He hit you because you're out doing what he can't." He looked her in the eye. "You're the one who's been keeping this family together."

Danielle shook her head as she lowered her eyes to the ground "I can't do it anymore. I can't carry him. I need a life too."

Nate stood up, dragging her to her feet. He pulled her into his arms and hugged her tightly. "Yes you do."

"Oh God!" she cried again on his chest, "What am I going to do now?"

Nate pulled her back and kissed her on the forehead. "You're going to do just as you planned to do. I'm going to take care of your brother and you're going to have the time of your life."

"But...but," she stuttered.

"No buts!" He grinned. "I have another meeting that I couldn't get out of, so I'm going to drop you off at my place. You take a shower, maybe a nap, and then get in that sexy dress and we'll have a nice dinner when I get home."

Nate dropped Danielle off at his home. He showed her a room that she could use while she was with him. And even gave her a shirt of his in case she needed something to sleep in.

Danielle did end up taking a long hot bath instead of a shower. With the crying that she did and with all the tension suddenly gone from her body she found that she couldn't resist the call to the bed. Pulling the covers back she crawled in with only her panties on. Within seconds she was out, sleeping hard.

44

That was how Nate found her. He walked into her room to wake her for dinner but found her sleeping on her stomach with her arms under the pillows and one leg bent at the knee. It seemed that as she slept she had kicked all of the covers off. He got a nice view of her rear covered in the thin lace panties he bought for her.

Nate walked up to the bed and sat down softly next to her. With the back of his hand he touched her bare back. Lightly he trailed it down her spine to the fullness of her backside. She was soft, so silky, that he itched to touch all of her. To kiss each sweet spot and then some. Instead he trailed his hand down the back of her leg to the sheet, where he gently pulled it up.

Brushing her hair way from her face, Nate leaned down and kissed the cheek that was still slightly red. "Sleep tight," he said softly, "You're going to need it."

Chapter Five

Danielle woke up around nine. She found her clothes folded on top of the oak dresser. Draped on the chair next to the dresser, was a new set of clothes, pale blue slacks along with a matching sleeveless sweater. Soft leather shoes, with low heels, were on the floor next to the chair. She dressed in the clothes and quickly found Nate sitting out in the back on the balcony reading a paper and eating breakfast.

"Well morning, sunshine." Nate grinned at her over his paper.

Danielle blushed. "Sorry about dinner. Guess I was a lot more tired than what I thought."

"Oh don't worry about it." He folded his paper up and sat up straight in his chair. "We'll have other dinners."

"Thanks for the clothes."

"All part of my royal treatment. Want some breakfast?"

Danielle shook her head as she sat down. "I don't think I could eat a thing." She blushed again when she looked up at him. "My stomach is kind of nervous."

"Well at least have some juice. We have a very busy day ahead of us."

She watched him pour some of the orange juice in her glass. "You don't have to work?"

Nate shrugged his shoulders. "Oh, I'm supposed to." When he looked up at her his eyes sparkled, "But since I do own the company I've decided that I'm going to take some time off."

"Can you do that?" She took a sip of her juice, watching him closely.

Nate took a deep breath. "I've found that in this position I can do just about anything I want."

"Or buy anything you want?" She gave him a bland look, but her eyes held a challenge.

"Sometimes." He gave her the same look she gave him.

After a lengthy stare down in silence, Danielle put her face into her hands and groaned, "Oh, why do I feel like this is all a big mistake?"

"Because for the first time ever you're not in control." He didn't smile when she looked up at him. "I am."

"Nate, I really don't…" she started to say but stopped when he slid a folder over to her. "What's this?"

"Our contract." He opened the folder to one page only. "All you have to do is read over it, and sign."

She looked up, showing him with her eyes how scared she was suddenly. "That's it?"

"That's it," he replied with his all business voice.

"I sign this and all of my brother's medical problems disappear," she said softly to herself. Along with my heart, she finished in her head.

Danielle took a deep breath and quickly signed the contract after she read over it. Everything read just as they had talked about it. For staying with Nate for two weeks he would provide all medical care for her brother.

Nate took the folder back quickly. "Now that's out of the way we can get started on our day."

"And what do you have in mind?" Her heart started to pound as her mind suddenly put pictures in her head.

"Relax, Dannie." He smiled. "All I had planned so far was taking you out shopping."

"Shopping?" She frowned back, not understanding.

"Yes, shopping," he chuckled, standing up and taking her hand, "If I'm going to take you out and show you off then you're going to need the best clothes that money can buy." He kissed her hand, giving her the most charming smile. "I plan on knocking them snobs on their asses."

Nate ended up spending a small fortune on Danielle. He bought ten pairs of slacks in almost every color, and included matching silk tops and sweaters, name brand jeans and sneakers. Nate selected cocktail dresses, a strapless red, an off the shoulder white, and finally a tight black dress with an open back, and a plunging neckline in the front. Each dress had a matching pair of high heels.

Nate did break for lunch, taking her back to the same restaurant where they'd had their first meeting. This time when Danielle sat down she didn't see anyone staring.

"It is so funny how a set of clothes can make all the difference," she told Nate as she looked over her menu.

"True, but they're still snobs." He smiled.

Danielle laughed, "If you can't stand your own kind, then why do you live like this?"

"That's a good question. But first what would you like?"

She grinned at him as she put her menu down. "Promise you won't laugh?"

"No." He smiled.

Danielle shook her head. "I want a simple hamburger with cheese fries and a coke."

"Ah." The waiter walked up to them just as Nate put his own menu down. "A woman after my own heart."

"My I take your order?" the waiter asked.

Nate wiggled his eyes at Danielle before he looked at the man. "Two burgers, cheese fries, and two cokes." The waiter looked at Nate as if he might have lost his mind.

"We don't have that, Sir."

"You know what?" Danielle asked Nate, "I have a better idea."

She took his hand and pulled him out of his chair. Laughing, they walked out of the restaurant and back into the car.

"Mind telling me where we're going?" he asked.

"I'm going to take you to the best burger joint around." She smiled back at him.

An hour later Nate had to admit that the small diner, in a part of town where he normally wouldn't eat, did have the best burgers. He also found that he was enjoying himself even more than what he expected. Just spending time with her was enough for Nate to realize exactly what he was missing in his life.

Back in the car, Nate took Danielle to one last store. *Fredrick's of Hollywood.* It was one of the best places to shop for lingerie. He smiled brightly when her face turned beet red as he picked out things she needed, and things she didn't need, but he wanted to see her wearing.

Nightgowns, silks robes, panties in all colors and some thongs. Bras, strapless and with straps. Stockings in matching colors to go with the panties along with garters and a few teddies just to deepen her blush. The final deal that made her so uncomfortable was when he put his foot down and told her she had to go into the dressing room and try on the cream silk baby doll.

So standing in front of the mirror in the dressing room with only the baby doll lingerie on, Danielle stared at herself. She couldn't get over the sudden change in her appearance or how sexy she looked. She also had to admit to herself that she loved how the silk felt against her skin.

However, Danielle got the shock of her life when Nate suddenly appeared behind her in the dressing room.

"What are you doing?" she cried out in a hushed voice.

Nate grinned as he watched her try to cover her body with her arms. "I thought I would come in and see if the color suits you." He stood as close to her backside as he could. With gentle, but firm hands, he pulled her arms away. He captured her eyes in the mirror with his own. "And it does."

"You can't be in here," she exclaimed, her eyes bulging. "What if someone sees you?"

"What if they do?"

Danielle watched him in the mirror closely. She saw the hunger in his eyes and it both scared the hell out of her and excited her to death. Danielle used to dream that Nate Remington would look at her just as he was now.

"Nate!"

"Shhh," he whispered in her ear softly, "I want to look at you." His eyes captured hers, "Really look at you."

Danielle had the strong desire to close her eyes and lean back against him, but something in his eyes stopped her from doing just that. His hand slid up and down her arms before they moved down her legs. He touched as much of them as he could from where he stood behind her.

"You're so soft," he said as he rubbed his face into her hair, never breaking eye contact, "And you smell so good."

When his arms wrapped around her waist and pulled her back against him in a tight hold, Danielle closed her eyes and sighed in bliss. "This isn't the place to be doing this."

Nate moved some of her hair from her neck using his chin. He kissed a spot next to her neck. "Then maybe we should hurry up so we can finish this at home."

Danielle opened her eyes quickly and looked at him in the mirror with shock all over her face. She watched helpless as his hand flattened over her stomach, under the top of her baby doll. Butterflies started in the pit of her stomach while she watched his hands slowly move up under the top. Her mouth went dry when the first tips of his fingers touched the underside of her breasts.

"Nate!" she gasped. Her hands went up to stop his as someone suddenly knocked on the dressing room door.

"Is everything alright in there?" one of the clerks asked.

Danielle turned around quickly and looked up at Nate scared to death. "What do we do?" she asked him in a hushed whisper.

Nate grinned, hugging her., "Answer her."

"Yes," she answered, looking at Nate. "I'll be out in a few moments."

Nate leaned down and kissed her lightly on the mouth. He smiled at her when he was done and when she looked at him. "I'll be waiting."

* * * *

Back at the house Nate helped Danielle bring all the bags into her room. On a whim, while Danielle was unpacking her things, Nate told her to shower and dress in the white dress. Tonight they were going out for dinner and dancing.

Danielle showered quickly, taking extra time with fixing her hair so the sides were pulled back, but small curls hung on the sides. Standing only in a towel she went to work on her make-up, not expecting Nate to show up in her room. He did.

"Oh, sorry," he said from the door, "I thought you would have been ready by now."

Danielle jumped and turned around suddenly. Her hand went right to the knot at the top of her breast as she looked at him, "I...um, sorry. I'm almost ready."

Nate had to swallow hard while he looked at her. "No problem. I'll...um...I'll just wait for you."

Danielle had to wait a few minutes for her nerves to settle down before she could finish her make-up. Just to be safe as she dressed, she locked the bedroom door, something that she should have done to begin with.

She hung the dress she was planning on wearing tonight on the back of the door. Sitting on the bed she slid the see through white panties up her legs. The next thing was the white garter belt, then the pale tan stockings. No bra was needed tonight because of the style of the dress. Nate had picked out the tight white dress with elbow length sleeves that had a low cut bodice that draped off her shoulders

Danielle managed to get half of the dress zipped up the back, the rest she couldn't reach. So slipping into her white heels, Danielle walked out of the room in search of Nate.

"Hey Nate," she called out as she worked on an earring, "Can you help me get this dress zipped the rest of the way?"

"Oh wow!" Nate looked at Danielle as if he was seeing his first real woman. "That dress..."

Danielle giggled, "Needs zipping up." She walked up to him and turned around, "Please?"

"I would prefer the zipper going down." He gave her a mischievous smile when she turned her head around and looked at him, "But we do have a dinner to go to."

In the car Danielle kept blushing and laughing. Nate was looking at her every couple of blocks.

"Stop it!" she laughed.

"I can't help it," he chuckled back, "You look gorgeous."

Danielle blushed at him and Nate quickly moved. He kissed her so fast that Danielle didn't have time to brace herself for it.

His hands held her face in place while his lips moved over hers gently. It was a simple kiss, but it spoke loudly.

Nate wanted her, and he wanted to make sure Danielle knew it.

Reluctantly he stopped kissing her when the car pulled up to the restaurant. Quickly Nate got out of the car and rushed to her side, helping her out. Hand in hand they walked up to the front door.

The restaurant was packed. Nate explained to her that it was always like this. It was one of the most popular places for eating because you could dance afterwards. Getting a table required reservations to be made months in advance. Nate just smiled when Danielle asked him how he got a table so quickly.

At their table, Nate looked at his watch and smiled. "Perfect timing." When Danielle frowned at him in a questioning manner and he grinned at her. "We have at least two hours before the band plays."

"Two hours?" she exclaimed, "Do you really think we're going to be here that long?"

"Oh I know it," he chuckled. Looking up as a waiter poured water into their glasses, he added, "With it being this packed it will at least take us one hour just to eat our food." Another waiter came over with an ice bucket that had a bottle of red wine chilling in it. "And you must save room for their chocolate cake. Their cake is the best in the city."

Danielle smiled as he poured her wine in the glass. "Chocolate cake?"

"It's lip smacking good!" He smiled back.

Forty-five minutes later two large platters of lobsters were placed in front of them, along with salads, a bowl of roasted potatoes and fresh baked bread hot from the oven. Nate watched her with pleasure as she ate the food.

True to his word, an hour and a half later a large piece of chocolate cake sat before her. It was the best cake she had ever tasted. She closed her eyes as the treat melted over her tongue.

"I told you it was the best." He grinned at her.

"That you did," she moaned, licking her lips.

Watching Danielle lick her lips was a sweet torture for Nate. His body responded suddenly and need for her hit hard. To have waited so long to be near her and now to wait until she was ready was killing him. Nate didn't think he could wait much longer to really touch her like he wanted to.

By the time another bottle of red wine was served the music was playing. Nate stood up, taking Danielle by the hand. He led her out to the dance floor, joining others dancing, and pulled her into his arms.

"Is this why you wine and dine?" she giggled up at him.

"Why?" he charmed back, "Is it working?"

Danielle laughed in a carefree manner as he moved them around the dance floor, "Oh I could get used to this."

After almost an hour of dancing they took a break for more wine and a sample of some chocolate truffles. Danielle told him the only chocolate she ever got was the box one bought around Valentine's Day.

After another hour of dancing and laughing, it was around midnight by the time they headed back to Nate's home. Danielle snuggled up on his shoulder tired and a little tipsy from all the wine. Her feet were also killing her from all the dancing they had done while wearing her new shoes.

Once home, Nate sat her down on the sofa in the living room at the back of the house. He knelt down in front of her, pulling her shoes off and rubbing her sore feet.

"So I will assume that you enjoyed yourself tonight?" he asked with the charming smile on his face that Danielle was starting to get used to.

"I never knew that people could live like that. Dancing, the great food…" She gave a big sigh. "Sure is nice to have the money to do all of that."

"Yes, but if you don't have someone to share it with, then why bother." He moved to the other foot, keeping his blue eyes fixed on her.

"I'm sure that you have had dates that you enjoyed," she joked.

"Some," he agreed, massaging her calves as he talked, "But for some reason I find I can enjoy these things better with you."

Danielle looked at him and again felt the butterflies in her stomach. Having him so close and knowing what he wanted scared the hell out of her. Danielle knew that if she let him, this man would break her heart to the point of never fixing it.

"Well, um, I think I'm going to call it a night." She pulled her legs from his lap, picked up her shoes, and stood up. "It really was a great night."

Nate watched her go and chastised himself for not calling out or going after her. He didn't want her sleeping down the hall from him. Nate wanted Danielle in his bed, in his arms.

"Night Dannie," he said softly.

In her room, Danielle tossed her shoes to the side and went to work taking the earrings and bracelet off. When she went to work at unzipping her dress she found that she couldn't reach it.

"Shit!" she mumbled as she tried again to twist around. But the dress was so tight that there was no way it was going to work.

So in her stocking covered feet Danielle walked out of her bedroom and down to Nate's room. Instead of knocking on the door like she should have, Danielle just walked in. Her head was down as she still tried to work at catching the zipper of her dress.

"Nate, can you give me a hand?" When she looked up at him, Danielle got a shock.

Nate was standing at the foot of his bed with only his slacks on. His jacket, shirt and tie were draped over a chair and it looked like he just finished taking his shoes and socks off. In fact, Danielle noticed right off that if she would have came a few seconds later she would have caught him with his pants down. His slacks were unbuttoned and unzipped, barely hanging onto his hips. They were also showing the top outline of his tight briefs.

"Oh, I'm sorry!" she gasped, looking him up and down, not being able to stop herself from looking. "I should have knocked first."

Nate's body responded suddenly to her looking him over. His cock pressed against the front of his pants and his hands fisted and unfisted. "No problem," he rasped out. Clearing his throat he went on, "What do you need?"

Danielle swallowed hard. "I…um…I can't reach my zipper again," she stuttered out.

"Turn around." His voice seemed to thicken as he spoke. It was something that Danielle noticed.

She turned her back on him and bit her lower lip the second she felt his hot hands on her back. Her eyes closed as the zipper slowly moved down her back. Heart suddenly pounding in her chest, Danielle found she couldn't move. She couldn't walk away and go back to her room like she knew she needed to.

Her breath suddenly caught in her throat when Nate's hands flattened on her back, spreading her dress as wide as it would go. Slowly her eyes opened as he turned her around to face him. She looked up helplessly when using one hand he brushed his knuckles across her cheek.

"You are so beautiful," he whispered.

"Nate," she whispered back, watching as his head lowered down to her own.

Chapter Six

Nate kissed Danielle deeply. His hands went to her shoulders, pulling her closer to his bare chest. Deeper still the kiss went as his tongue darted in her mouth gently. He touched her tongue and moaned his pleasure.

He pulled at her dress until her breasts, feeling the panic in her. She started to struggle slightly which only helped him to pull her dress down to her waist. It also caused his pants to drop down to his ankles.

Nate let her break out of his embrace and watched her take a step back, only to sit down hard at the foot of the bed. He watched her with hungry eyes as she crossed her arms over her bare breasts. Keeping eye contact he kicked his slacks away from his legs and knelt down in front of her.

On his knees, Nate found he was determined to see her. To touch her skin and kiss every sweet inch of the body that haunted his dreams every night. Never taking his eyes off of Danielle, his hands went to her dress that was bunched up around her waist, and as slowly as he could stand it, Nate pulled the dress down and off her body.

His breath caught in his own throat at seeing her sitting on his bed in nothing more than her white garter belt, stockings and white panties, the color of purity Nate's cock sprang to life and almost hurt he was so hard from thinking about her innocence.

Touching her cheek again and running his finger tips along her jaw line up to her lips, Nate whispered, "You are so beautiful."

Nate never gave Danielle a chance to do anything. He leaned up on his arms that were now on the bed next to her and kissed her. This kiss was filled with hungry need. The need that only she would be able to fulfill. His hands pulled her arms away as his chest came down on hers. Quickly he had them both in the center of the bed with his body covering hers. Using his legs, Nate was able to get between hers and the feel of her soft body under his hardness was unspeakable. He could not put into words to save his life what it felt like to be this close, and yet he needed to get much closer to her. Nate felt that if he didn't he wouldn't be able to breathe any longer.

Nate kissed her deeply, devouring her mouth while his body rubbed on hers, groaning the moment her arms went around his body, loving each and every slow minute of it all. His hands roamed over her body as his tongue did a dance of its own with hers.

Heated lips kissed a trail away from her lips and moved down her jaw to her neck. He kissed her shoulder, and then licked back up to the earlobe. All the while this was going on his hands went to work unclasping the stockings from the garter belt. The moment both sets were free Nate pushed his way down her body.

He licked, and then kissed a fiery trail down to one bare breast. His tongue darted out; lightly taking a swipe at her hard nipple. As he sucked it into his mouth he looked up at Danielle. Her eyes were closed and she was panting with every breath. As soon as he had the whole thing in his mouth she arched her back up towards him, inviting him to take more.

Nate rolled the hard peak with his tongue, lightly giving it bites. Popping the one breast out of his mouth he moved over to the next. At the same time his hand slid down her side, skimming between their bodies. He slipped his hand inside her panties, touching first the small patch of curls then the bare mound of her pussy. Nate moaned against her flesh at the feel of the wet heat that greeted his hand.

Nate rubbed his hand over the mound as he rubbed his body over hers. Not once did he slip a finger inside her like he wanted. His plan was to get her so hot that when the time came for her to lose control she would do it screaming.

Removing his hand he braced his body over hers, kissing and licking his way down. He grinned as he did this, mostly because her breathing became ragged and fast. When he reached her belly he stopped and looked up at her.

Nate caught her eyes and held them. He saw the fright, the need, and something else he wasn't too sure about. He picked up one leg and slowly rolled the stocking down her thigh. The moment her ankle was bare he kissed it, licking his way up to her knee before he let the leg go. Nate did the same thing to her other leg, enjoying the sounds she made when she lost her breath.

Carefully his hand hooked onto the garter belt and the hem line of her panties. He watched her watching him as he pulled the pair down her legs. Not wanting to break the spell that weaved between them, Nate slowly moved off the bed and pulled his briefs down his legs.

He stood at the foot of the bed a few moments letting Danielle get her first view of a man's naked body in all its glory. He didn't show her any emotion when she looked at his face with shock filled eyes.

Nate crawled back onto the bed, scooting her up more into the center before he came down on his elbows. He settled himself between her legs with his head by her belly.

"Don't be scared," he told her softy, "I would never hurt you." He kissed her belly. "I need you. I need to touch you everywhere."

Danielle dug her hands into the sheets as he kissed his way down her body. Hot breath touched wet skin. It was enough for her to tense up under him, waiting to see what was coming next.

"Relax, Dannie," he told her, "I'm only going to love you."

The first swipe of his tongue between the heated slit had her almost bucking under him. Danielle started to breathe so hard and so fast she thought she was going to hyperventilate and pass out. The second swipe had her seeing stars.

Nate worked off of her body language and dove into her as if he was a kitten getting his first taste of sweet cream. He licked long and slow. Taking in each drop of her honey that she had to give, and then licking until he got some more. When he glanced up at her as his tongue was moving in tiny circles around her hard clit, Danielle's eyes closed. Tiny droplets of sweat beaded her brow and a frown covered her eyes as he wound her up tighter.

He gave her one more long lick before he moved his mouth, replacing it with his hand. Nate licked his way up her body, planting kisses everywhere. He slipped two fingers inside her, rubbing her hard clit with his thumb.

Nate watched her face in painful bliss as he brought her to the first orgasm of the night. Her mouth opened, eyes closed, and back arched up as the pleasure washed over her.

As she rode the wave, Nate moved into position. His hand was still between their bodies, moving and building her up for more. He kissed one of her breasts, sucking the nipple hard into his mouth before he moved up to her neck. Danielle's hands went around his waist as yet another orgasm suddenly hit her. Nate used this to position the head of his cock at her tight entrance. She moaned the pleasure against his shoulder as he pushed his way inside. The after shocks that hit the sensitive tip almost pushed him over.

Closing his eyes tightly, Nate pushed more inside her. His teeth gritted at how tight she was. He still found it hard to believe that after all this time she was still a virgin. How could she have held onto such a treasure for so long?

"Nate!" Danielle cried out, nails digging into his back.

Nate worked hard to block out the pain on his back as he pushed through the thin tissue that was her innocence. It didn't give easy so force was needed, but the reward he felt traveled down his spine at being so deeply embedded inside her was worth it. He touched her so deeply that he could swear he could feel the pounding of her heart all through out his own body.

Nate forced his body to stay put, to hold onto this feeling as long as he could. But he had to open his eyes and look at her. He had to see her face. See the expression in her beautiful eyes as he stayed so still while he was deep inside her body. The body he not only dreamed about for years, but the body that no other man has ever touched.

Green, tear filled eyes looked up at the emotion filled blue ones. Nate watched a single tear slip out and down her cheek. It was a tear he couldn't tell if it was from the emotions in the room or from the pain of this being her first time.

With all the tenderness he had, Nate lowered his body all the way down to hers. He braced some of the weight on his elbows as he kissed the tear. He tried to kiss all of her pain away. He wanted to take everything away and only give her the happiness that he knew deep down she deserved.

Lips touched as he moved. He nipped, and then rubbed his lips against hers while his hips started a steady motion. Slowly he withdrew only to thrust back in. Each plunder in caused Danielle to catch her breath, and before long she was matching him.

She wrapped her legs tightly around his hips as he moved. Soon Nate was thrusting inside her with eyes closed tightly. Balls started to tighten and chills raced down his spine way too early for him. He fought within himself to hold out longer. To give Dannie one more orgasm before it all ended.

"One more, Dannie," he groaned, rearing back some with his eyes still shut tightly, "Just come with me one more time."

Danielle shook her head no, but she also had her eyes closed. He decided, she was hanging onto him as tightly as she could, feeling the ultimate pleasure just finger tips away.

Nate also felt it.

He rotated his hips to bump her clit just right. It was all she needed. Danielle screamed and nails dug into the cheeks of his ass. Nate also cried out. The tight muscles in her pussy contracted around his cock, taking all his strength and draining him dry. He reared back on his hands while his orgasm slammed hard into him.

Moments passed but it felt like hours as he stayed put, waiting for it all to end. Yet, Nate knew this was all just the beginning. Now that he had a taste of the treasure that was all Danielle, he didn't know if he wanted to give it up. Didn't know if he would be able to sleep in the bed without her.

Hours later he was lying on his side, Dannie in his arms in the spoon position sleeping. Nate was not. He had his head resting on the pillow above hers, thinking. His arms were wrapped around her tightly. Fingers linked with hers, his body was as content as it could be, and yet his mind was not. As he held the one girl that gave him the hottest dreams in his arms, Nate was wondering what was going to happen after the two weeks were up? It was a question he was afraid to find the answer to.

* * * *

Nate woke up alone in the bed around noon. His arm reached out for Danielle but instead of her warm body next to his he touched a piece of paper. His eyes snapped opened quickly as the worst thought crossed his mind. Danielle left and is not coming back.

I didn't have the heart to wake you. You looked so peaceful sleeping. I went into the hospital to check on Paul. The doctor told me on the phone that my father came in trying to change things again. Hope to be back by noon. Dannie

Nate tossed the sheet off of his body, heading for the shower. He thought that if she was supposed to be back at noon then things weren't going as well at the hospital as he had hoped.

He dressed quickly in a pair of jeans, t-shirt, and sneakers. After a forty-five minute drive that felt like hours, Nate arrived at the hospital. When he stepped off the elevator on the third floor and spotted the first nurse he knew right away that something was wrong.

"Oh, Mr. Remington!" a woman in a business suit came rushing up to him. Nate thought he knew the woman, but couldn't put his finger on her, "I'm so glad you showed up."

"I don't mean to be rude, but I'm not here for any kind of business. I'm here to find someone," he told her, looking around the wing for any signs of Danielle.

"Yes, I know," she told him, looking like she didn't have a clue as to what to do, "I just received the memo about Paul Hughes. I'm so sorry. We haven't been able to change anything yet."

Nate looked at her with a frown on his face. His gut told him that something was wrong, "He hasn't been moved yet?"

"Well," she swallowed hard, "We were in the process of moving him when his father showed up. And I must add the man seems to be drinking. He started to make a scene when his daughter also showed up."

"Where are they?" Fear grabbed Nate. He knew what Robert Hughes had done to his daughter and that was just from him having a date with her. If the man was drunk and ran into Dannie he feared what would happen.

"We managed to get them into one of the private rooms the doctors go to give families bad news." She looked over her shoulder. "Mr. Hughes locked the door and we're waiting for security now."

Nate took off at a run down the hall. He found the room mostly because there were nurses standing by the door.

"Dannie!" he yelled through the door.

"How could you!"

Nate could hear Robert yelling at Danielle. It not only put more fear into him but it also built up his anger.

"I'm not doing any of this for you!" Danielle screamed back.

"You are nothing but an ungrateful bitch!"

"Stand back," Nate told the group of nurses. He took a step back then with all his might kicked the door in. It was then that he saw Robert backhand Danielle so hard she went flying into the wall. She screamed and started crying with the shock and pain, Nate saw red.

Danielle closed her eyes and cried hard as she slid down the wall on her shoulder to the floor. She never even saw Nate burst into the room, or rushing over and grabbing her father by the back of his shirt. The only thing that she felt, besides being numb, was unloved. All she ever wanted was one small piece of her father's love.

Security came running into the room while Nate struggled with Robert. Between the three of them they managed to tackle him to the ground and cuff him.

Nate rushed over to Danielle who was still on the floor crying. He saw right away the mark from Robert hitting her so hard. This time he feared it was going to leave a small bruise.

He pulled her into his arms, letting her cry on his shoulder. He watched Robert being dragged out of the room. He didn't understand how a man could love only one child when he had two. Hell he didn't even understand his own father.

"Come on," he said to her, "Let's get you home."

"What about Paul," she sobbed, "I never got to see him."

"Do you really want your brother to see you like this?"

Danielle looked up at him and laughed along with her crying, "What am I going to do?"

"You're going to come home with me." He gave her a tender smile. "Let me take care of everything."

Back at the house, Danielle went to soak in the bath while Nate took care of some business on the phone. Danielle ended up crying some more and Nate fixed them a light lunch.

By the time she came out in one of her new satin robes, Nate had the small table in the kitchen set up waiting.

"Better?" Nate asked with a kind smile on his face.

Danielle sat down across from him. With her head down, she fought a new set of tears that threatened to fall. "Not really." When she did look up at him the tears fell. "Why doesn't he love me?"

"Probably the same reason my father never cared for me." Nate grinned, taking her hand in his. "I know you want his love, Dannie. And I wish I could give it to you. I also know that what I'm about to say wont be much help to you but there is a time when you have to stop, just like I did. You're going to have to stop trying to get what he will never give." He kissed her hand. "You're going to have to stop and say that this is my life. It's time I live it as I want."

Danielle pulled her hand away and sniffed back her tears. She quickly wiped them away from her face and put on a smile for him. "You're right. I need to stop wondering why and start living."

Nate wasn't buying her sudden light hearted attitude. He watched her closely but couldn't see what he thought was there. She pushed all the pain away and stood back up.

"Where you going?" he asked.

"I...um...I," she stuttered as she walked past him.

Nate reached out and grabbed her arm. He yanked her down on his lap. Both hands went to her face, forcing her to look at him, "You don't have to go through this alone," he told her in his soft, caring voice.

"You don't understand," she told him in barely a whisper, "I'm always alone."

Nate released her and she stood back up. He didn't watch her walk out of the room. He just sat there looking at the empty spot where she had been sitting, thinking about what she'd said.

An hour later, Danielle came into the living room dressed with her hair up in a pony tail. She was back in jeans and seemed to look like the same Dannie Nate liked.

"What's up?" he asked, putting his paper down.

"We're going to do something different tonight," she said.

"And what might that be?"

"Tonight we're going to get a few movies, sit in our sweats, and eat nothing but junk food." She grinned at him, tugging him out of the chair by his hand.

"Sounds like a plan to me," he laughed.

"Good. And there's only one rule." She tossed his jacket at him.

"And what might that be?"

Danielle held the door open for him, "No business calls."

At the rental store, Nate had fun joking with Danielle over movies. He wanted to get a new action movie and she wanted something scary. When he picked up a sexy adult movie and mentioned it she hit him in the shoulder. In the end they both got the movie that they wanted, and only once did his cell phone ring. As he was looking at the caller id during check out, Danielle snatched it from his hands. She reminded him of their deal and slipped it into her pocket.

Before they left the store it rang again and Nate ended up wrestling it away from her. He didn't answer it, but wanted to know who called him.

With smiles on their faces both set up a junk food picnic on the living room floor. Danielle reminded Nate that he also had to go and put on his sweats—dress as some would say 'slobs' Danielle turned the lights off while Nate put the action movie in to play first.

They started out on the sofa watching the movie, but halfway into it they were sitting on the floor engrossed in the movie. It was something that Nate hadn't done in a very long time. However, things changed. The phone rang again and this time Nate answered it. He stood off to the side with his cell talking as Danielle sat on the floor with a strange look on her face. They were in the middle of the second movie and he was on the phone. It was something that she wasn't going to put up with. Not tonight.

Standing up she walked over to Nate. He gave her an 'I'm sorry' look along with a shrug of his shoulders.

"We have a deal," she hissed at him.

"I didn't answer for a reason," he said in the phone. Then covering the mouth piece he said to Danielle in a hushed voice, "I'm sorry. I'll wrap this up as fast as I can."

"Oh, I've a strong feeling I can help you along there." She gave him an evil grin and walked behind him.

Nate thought that she was going to head to bed, so when his sweat pants suddenly came down to his ankles he didn't know what to do. It was the first time anyone had caught him off guard like that and the first time he was de-pantsed since high school.

"Yep, still has that nice ass," she told him right before she landed a swat to it.

"I'll call you back later," Nate said hastily into the phone, and then hung up. He looked at her with a steely-eyed expression "Oh you are going to pay for that."

Danielle backed away, giggling. "Sure you don't need to make a call first?"

"I'll show you make a call—" He bent over, pulling the sweats off his ankles and kicking them away. "After I get a hold of you."

Chapter Seven

Danielle backed away from Nate with a mischievous grin on her lips. She had a dare in her eyes and a challenge that Nate was ready to meet. He walked toward her slowly, giving her the same smile that she had for him. However, Danielle wasn't ready for him to lunge after her.

She screamed in laughter as she turned and ran from him. She headed right into the kitchen, putting the table between them. When she moved left, Nate moved also. He had an evil grin on his face and looked like he was more than ready to capture her.

"You know you're not going to win. When I get my hands on you…"

"You'll what?" she challenged back.

Nate looked her up and down licking his lips. "Oh, baby, you'll just have to find out the hard way."

"You know what the trouble with little rich boys like you is," she taunted, "You're all talk with very little action."

"You're going to see some action now."

Nate pulled his shirt up over his head and Danielle took that small distraction and ran out of the kitchen. Nate was right behind her. He expected Danielle to run into her room, so when she went for the stairs he was surprised. His office and an extra room were up there, nothing much for her to hide from him. He managed to catch her around the waist and gave an evil laugh at her squeal.

"Got you!"

Nate picked her up.

"Unfair!" she yelled, struggling in his arms.

He only laughed at her, walked back down and headed for the bedroom. At the bottom of the stairs he turned her around and suddenly flung her over his shoulder.

"Hey!" she screamed at him, "This isn't fair!"

"You already said that," Nate said and chuckled while he opened the door to his room. "I don't recall any rules being stated here."

Nate walked up to his bed and tossed Danielle on it. He laughed at her as she flipped over onto her back and he prepared himself for another chase. He wasn't prepared, however, for what she did do.

Danielle came up on her knees in front of him. She raked her nails up his chest and stood as she went higher. Standing up on the bed, she hung her arms over his shoulders, bent slightly and kissed him.

Nate wrapped his arms around her, kissing her back. Fingers went to work at pulling her sweats down her legs, and then she stepped out of them. Things quickly changed then. Her kisses became more demanding and she pressed her body closer.

Nate ended up picking her up. He groaned in her mouth as she wrapped her legs around his waist. He turned around, sitting down on the bed with her in his arms. For just a quick moment he stopped kissing her in order to pull her shirt over her head. Nate felt his need rise quickly. He worked fast at taking her bra off, yet that still wasn't enough. He wanted and needed to be inside her. To feel the sweet hug of her flesh wrapped around his aching cock.

So standing up again, and still kissing her, he pulled his briefs down his legs. When he sat down once more he groaned in frustration. He'd forgotten to take Danielle's panties off.

"I'll buy you more," he told her with his mouth still touching hers.

"What?"

Nate ripped the thin material from her body and pushed two fingers deep inside her. Danielle moaned, tossing her head back as he kissed her throat. She held onto his shoulders as her hips moved over his hand. The pleasure was so intense she felt as if she was going to burst into flames any moment.

"You like that?" Nate asked her as his tongue left a hot trail up her throat to her jaw, "I have more to give if you think this rich boy has enough in him to give you the action you were talking about?" Nate removed his hand, taking hold of the hard flesh between his legs. He rubbed the head of his cock along her wet slit, smiling at how she was trying to get it inside her, "Ah, so you do want that?"

Danielle ran her hands in his hair, fisting it in balls before she yanked his head back. Nate hissed from the pain but it was replaced quickly with a moan. She started to kiss, lick and nibble on his neck just the same way he had down her neck. Nate positioned the head, but held her hips. He prevented her from taking what she wanted. He wanted her to watch.

"Look, Dannie," he whispered, "Watch as you take me into your body."

Danielle looked down, just as he was. She watched as her body lowered onto him; watched as she took each and every lovely inch of his cock into her tight pussy. It seemed that with her watching, it heightened the pleasure that she was feeling. Before she had taken all of him Danielle had to close her eyes while a small orgasm shook her.

"Yeah," Nate moaned, "I love feeling you clamp down." Quickly he slammed her down the rest of the way. "Now give me more."

Green eyes watched blue eyes as hips started to move. Danielle moved with the help of his hands on her hips. She found that this position had him deeper inside, but also gave her some of the control. She could move as fast as she wanted and as sharply. When her eyes started to close, Nate stopped her.

"No!" he said urgently, "Don't close your eyes. I want to watch you. I want to see the look in your eyes as you come."

Danielle bit her lower lip and moved her hips again. She found a tempo that suited her. It was steady but very sharp. Each inward move had Nate sucking in his breath as well. Soon Danielle found she was fucking Nate hard and fast.

"Oh, yeah," he moaned, "Just like that." He groaned as he cupped one of her breasts hard. "Don't stop!"

Sweat developed between her breasts. Heavy breathing and the sound of slapping flesh was loud in the room. A sudden 'oh shit' from Danielle had Nate taking over completely. He stood up, holding her tightly as her climax hit. Before she had a chance to come down, Nate had her back on her feet and facing away from him. Danielle didn't have much time to look over her shoulder and wonder what he was doing when he pushed back inside of her from behind.

Something came over him then—something primal. He wanted to dominate Danielle. To take her to heights that one only dreamed about. To push her orgasm so high that she would think her feet would never touch the ground.

Nate pounded into her so fast and hard that Danielle couldn't keep her balance. He felt her tighten up around him and groaned back his own release. He wanted one more thing from her. One thing that he knew Dannie wouldn't dream of doing. The one and only reason Nate was going to do this was he wanted as much of her as he could get. He wanted to make damn sure that the next man who touched her would not match him.

Just the thought of the possibility of someone else touching her had jealousy running hot in his veins. Quickly, he pushed that thought from his mind and her cry of release replaced it. Nate held her tightly as she shook around him again. He rubbed his face in her hair, breathing hard and hurting with need.

Withdrawing from her, Nate wrapped one arm tightly around her waist. His other hand gripped his cock and rubbed the large mushroom head over the small puckered ring of her ass. Making sure he held her tight and that she wasn't going to move at all, Nate pushed against it. He gritted his teeth at how tight it was, and how it wouldn't give.

"Nate!" Danielle cried out, "Don't!" she tried to pull his arm away from her waist, but he held her in an iron grip.

"Just once," he told her with gritted teeth, "Relax. It will hurt if you don't."

"Nate, please!"

"Please what?" he groaned. "I want you, every way I can have you. I want your virgin **body,** every orifice, branding you as mine. Let me." he murmured. "Relax. I think you'll like this."

Nate thought his knees were going to buckle when she murmured, "All right."

Pressing forward, the head of his cock he pressed into her ass, with some effort, though he went slowly, not wanting to hurt her. Only when he was inside her to the hilt did he stop and work on his breathing. He needed to get some kind of control over himself or he would hurt her, and that was something he would rather die than do.

Slowly he pulled out, leaving the head fully intact, then slowly pushed back in. He heard her whimpering, and paused, with monumental effort. "You okay?" he gasped. Nate needed to finish this.

He waited for her reply, praying she wouldn't make him stop.

"Yes, it's just…well…strange feeling."

He leaned over and grinned against her hair. "Woman, you'll be the end of me, you know that?"

Her light laughter made him close his eyes thinking how he didn't want the two weeks to end. He found that he wanted to tie Danielle to his bed and keep her always. Hell! Just the thought of tying her down to his bed gave him an extra boost of dominance.

The split second Danielle relaxed Nate let loose. He took her like a man possessed. The man he was at this moment. He rode her until she was screaming under him for more. It was her begging, telling him that she was so close that drove Nate crazy.

Nate held onto her hips with both hands. He fucked her hard. Head back, bodies slapping, and Nate was in heaven. He was so close to his own release and knew that it would only take one thing from her to push him over.

Both arms hugged her tightly while his hips still pounded. One of his hands moved down between her legs, finding the hard clit. With quick stroking motions from his fingers Danielle became wild. She bucked under him suddenly, screaming. Her orgasm was so powerful that tears fell from her eyes.

It was all Nate needed.

His cock erupted hot and heavy as his own cry of pleasure matched her own. He held her still under him while his soul emptied everything he had. His whole body shook from the force of it.

"Oh God!" he mumbled, breathing hard and afraid to move.

Looking down at Danielle, he smiled as he flicked his hair from his eyes. Danielle was slumped over the bed. The only reason she was even on her feet was because Nate was still holding her tightly.

At one in the morning both were laying in the bed. Nate was on his back with Danielle snuggled up against his side. Her head rested on his shoulder, a hand on his stomach and their legs intertwined with each other. Sweat covered their bodies as part of the sheet only covered their hips. Nate rubbed her bare back fighting to keep his eyes open. In the process of getting her into bed he ended up loving her again.

"I'm so tired I don't think I could move for a week," Danielle yawned.

"Now don't say that," he chuckled with his own yawn, "I have tickets to a play tomorrow night." He looked down at her face and grinned. She was out cold. With a deep breath Nate also closed his eyes, enjoying the feel of his woman tucked under his arm.

* * * *

"Come on, sweetheart!" Nate called out, pacing the hall, "We're going to be late."

Danielle opened the door, hopping on one foot as she tried to get her shoe on. "I've told you before. You can't rush these things."

Nate stood still with his mouth open staring at Danielle. They were going to a play that he had to call in a favor for just to get the tickets. He was expecting her to dress in the sexy black tonight. Seeing her in the tight, strapless gown left him speechless.

Her gown was a rich red velvet. It was tight on the bust, pushing her breasts up and filling them out nicely. Tight around the waistline and snug all the way down her hips. High on the back was a long slit. It was the only thing that gave the ability to move at all. Danielle had her hair up in a loose French roll with ringlets hanging down the sides of her face, and she was fighting with slipping into a pair of red velvet heels.

"Shit, my purse," she mumbled to herself, dashing back into her room and coming out with a small hand held purse. When she finally looked up at Nate she was smiling brightly, "Well?"

Nate worked hard at composing his face and tapped his finger on his lip, "Very nice." He walked around her, looking up and down, "Yes, very nice. The color is great on you."

"Well I'm so glad you approve," she laughed. Danielle looked over her shoulder at him, giving Nate a stern expression, "I thought we were going to be late?"

"Well I was just thinking about this one present I have for you," he said and paused in front of her. All joking gone from his face, he added, "I was going to save it as a going away present, but I think tonight I should give it you."

Danielle frowned as he walked into his bedroom. "Nate. You've already given me so much. You really don't have to…." Her speech suddenly stopped when he came out with a small velvet box, opened. "Nathaniel Remington!" she breathed in shock, "What have you done?"

Nate took out a necklace that was a solid ruby heart with small diamonds surrounding it on a fine gold chain. He walked around her, slipping the necklace around her neck and fastening it. "Now you will always have a part of my heart," he whispered in her ear before he kissed her shoulder.

Danielle touched the cool stone at her throat as she looked into his blue eyes. She gave him a tender smile, not knowing what to say.

Nate grinned, taking her hand and kissing her wrist. "Now let's get going. We're already late."

Nate had made arrangements to take Danielle to the popular *River Dance*. They sat up in the balcony with a perfect view of the stage. Nate watched her closely as they sat down. He thought of her as a child getting to see things for the first time.

It brought so much happiness to him to know that he was the one putting the smile on her face.

Leaning over in his seat, Nate whispered, "Have I told you that you look good enough to eat in that dress?"

Danielle blushed, but didn't look at him. "Shh. I'm trying to listen."

Nate grinned, sitting back up in his seat. After a few more moments went by he leaned toward her again. "I want to take you away for a few days." When she finally looked at him he went on, "I only have a few days left. I want to take you away where no one will find us and spoil rotten, like you've never been spoiled before."

"Nate," she started to speak but he held his finger to her lips.

"Don't try to talk me out of it." His eyes lowered to her lips before they went back up to her eyes. "My mind is made up. I want to take you to a place where I can live out all of our fantasies."

Danielle's heart started to pound as she looked at Nate. His words were starting to excite her to a point that she really no longer wanted to be sitting in a room with all of these people. Nate also felt that way.

"Let's go." He stood up, taking her hand.

"But it isn't over!"

Nate pulled Danielle out of the box. "If I'm going to take you away for our last few days then we need to get started on our plans right now."

"Plans?"

Nate rushed her out of the building and into the car that was parked down the street. They headed back to his house. Tossing his jacket on a nearby table he headed for the stairs.

"I'm going to head up to the library to make our arrangements," he told her as he walked up. "I shouldn't be too long."

An hour later Nate still hadn't come down and Danielle just knew that he was on the phone doing some kind of business. Dressed in her new lingerie and robe, Danielle headed up to the library. She found Nate sitting in a leather chair next to the fireplace. A large fire was burning and all of the lights were off, cell phone against his ear His shoes and socks were also gone, along with the tie from around his neck.

Danielle walked up to him and sat down on his lap, resting her head on his shoulder. She sighed when all she got was a kiss on the forehead as he talked.

"I thought you were only going to be up here for a few minutes," she said in a whisper in his ear."

"I'm sorry," he whispered back, holding the mouth piece on the phone, "The office called about something important. I have to deal with it before we can go."

Danielle shifted her body and went to work at the top buttons on his shirt. She kissed his earlobe before her tongue went down to his neck. "I know," she whispered, "But not nearly sorry enough."

Nate suddenly stiffened in his chair and sat up straighter. He worked hard at thinking about the conversation and not on what her hands and mouth were doing. It was a hard task since she was driving him crazy. Nate had to take a deep breath when his shirt suddenly opened up and her mouth started to kiss around his collar bone.

Again he covered the mouth piece and spoke softly, "This isn't fair, Dannie."

Her tongue skimmed up his chest to his neck again while her hand started to work on the belt of his pants, "I'm learning that playing fair with you is not the way to get things done." She pulled the belt all the way out and tossed it behind her. "I want to see how much of your conversation you can keep up with."

Nate bit his lower lip when her hand pulled his slacks apart and brought his hard cock out in the open. He cleared his throat as she started to slowly stroke the heavy flesh. On a groan his head went back and eyes closed. He knew then that she was trying to kill him.

"No!" Nate suddenly cried, sitting up and snapping back to the phone call, "Everything is fine, Mike. What else is there to know?"

"Oh, so you're going to play hard ball, huh?" she said in his ear. "Then let's see if you can fight this and stay on your damn phone."

Danielle stood up from his lap and walked in front of him. She slipped her robe off her shoulders, showing him the cream silk baby doll lingerie that he saw in the dressing room. Danielle grinned when he closed his eyes, bit his lip, and shook his head in frustration.

Danielle went down on her knees between Nate's legs. She kept her mischievous grin on her lips while she stroked him again. However the teasing was short lived. Nate's eyes bulged out and his breath caught in his throat the moment Danielle kissed the tip of his cock.

"Dannie, don't you dare," he hissed.

Danielle closed her eyes and sucked his cock into her mouth. She moaned against him while her tongue danced on the underside. She sucked him in until the head touched the back of her throat before she pulled back, sucking even harder.

"Mike…I…um…I need to go," Nate swallowed hard as she went down on the flesh again. "You can handle it all while I'm gone." Nate quickly shut the phone off and dropped it to the floor. His head went back on a deep groan as she worked slowly on him, "Oh, fuck, Dannie! You're killing me!"

Danielle popped the head out. Licking her lips she smiled up at him. "Oh I do hope so."

Nate dug his hands into the arms of his chair as she went to work on him again. She sucked hard on his cock, moaning her pleasure. The only thing that Nate seemed to be able to do was sit there and try not to pass out from his heavy breathing.

Up and down her head bobbed and Nate was powerless to do a thing. Each time he looked down to watch her suck his cock into the heat of her mouth he felt like he was going to lose it. His climax was so close yet he was powerless to stop her. He wanted more, and yet he wanted it to stop.

"Oh, shit!" he moaned loudly, breathing hard, "Oh fuck! No more." His hips started to buck on their own while his balls suddenly tightened up. "Oh God! Argh!" Nate yelled as his cock erupted deep inside her mouth.

He held his body up slightly with his hands on the armrest. Head back, breaths coming in gasps and still his orgasm spilled out of him. He was so powerless to stop it. Too weak to do anything but ride the wave out. Not even when Danielle released him and scooted back to the skin rug in front of the fire did Nate open his eyes.

"That was soooooo good," he moaned. Nate dropped his head down and opened his eyes. "And so not nice."

Danielle only grinned at him. Her hands went up to the three large buttons on the top of her outfit. In a teasing manner she slipped them off. One by one, "So then I guess doing this wouldn't be nice either?"

Nate stood up, watching her with hungry eyes. He finished taking his shirt off, and then slid the slacks down his legs. His cock was hard again, standing proud and waiting for her. Nate's eyes were full of emotions as he looked down at Danielle. He watched in torturous anticipation as she slipped the bottoms down her legs. He even licked his lips when she spread her legs for him slightly.

"Tonight, Dannie, I'm going to love you until you can't move," he told her in a husky voice.

Chapter Eight

Danielle leaned back with her arms supporting her weight as she watched Nate come down to the floor with her. She grinned in a seductive manner as he flattened down between her legs. Her mouth opened, head went back and a sighing moan slipped out with the first heated kisses to her swollen clit. Danielle braced herself for the attack and ended up crying out as Nate ate at her pussy like a starving man.

He licked at her quickly, stopping only to suck on her clit hard a few times. She couldn't stop her hips from bucking as he shoved his tongue inside her as deep as he could go. Danielle was panting hard as she leaned on one arm. Her other hand she fisted into his hair, digging him into her harder as her orgasm was close at hand.

"Oh God yes!" she cried out, squirming under his onslaught, "Don't stop!"

Danielle cried out her release, pressing his face into her hard. Only when she started to come down from her high did she let him go. Nate moved quickly on his knees, bringing her up with him. He positioned her right over his cock and slammed her down upon him.

Nate groaned as he felt the after shocks of her pleasure. He moved her fast and hard on him, leaving Danielle barely hanging on. His mouth found her, thrusting his tongue deep into her mouth as he fucked her. Danielle broke off to cry out her pleasure while his lips trailed down her throat and still Nate never slowed down the pace. If anything he increased it. He felt, suddenly, as if something was starting to change. He didn't have time to dwell on it, however. Danielle screamed out and Nate lost it. Her whole body shook with her orgasm and this time Nate could feel it all. He even felt her womb contract around his cock.

Holding her in what seemed like a bear hug Nate closed his eyes and waited for his own pleasure to subside. When it did he slowly lowered both of them back down to the floor, but found that he couldn't let her go.

"Oh wow!" Danielle sighed, wrapping her arms and legs even tighter around him, "What was that?"

Nate took a deep, shaky breath as he nuzzled her neck. "No clue." He moved slightly to look up at her and grinned when he heard her moan from the shift. "But I wouldn't mind doing that again." Nate gently removed himself from her body and rolled over to lie on his back. He had a big smile on his face.

Nate's phone rang and Danielle sat up with a frown on her face, "Not again," she groaned.

"Well I'm planning on going out of town for a few days," Nate defended himself, crawling over to the phone, "So I do have to wrap a few things up." Danielle also moved and bit Nate suddenly on the ass. "Hey! What's that for?"

"I'm going back down stairs and if you're not down there to join me in fifteen minutes I'm going to sleep in my own room—alone." She gave him a look. "And the door will be locked."

Ten minutes later Nate was standing in the bedroom, breathing hard from running, and smiling as Danielle walked out of the bathroom wearing a towel. Danielle smiled and pulled her towel away from her body. Nate sucked his breath in at her beauty. In all of his dreams and fantasies he never thought that Danielle Hughes would be standing in his room, nude as the day she was born.

Nate picked her up as if she was a child. He pressed her back against the wall and kissed her deeply. He moaned into her mouth as she wrapped her legs and arms around his body. Nate found that when his body was this close to hers he couldn't stand not being inside her. He wanted to be as close as two people could be.

"You're a drug, Dannie," he said against her lips as he slid his cock deep inside her heated depth. "A drug that keeps me coming back over and over again."

Danielle moved her hips on him as much as she could. One hand went up to his jaw as her eyes closed in bliss, "Stop talking."

Nate smiled before he kissed her again. His hips pounded into her quickly. Nate kept thinking that as frequently as the two of them were having sex that he should be lasting longer than this. But he was wrong. Each time they came together and each time her hunger rose up to match his, Nate knew he didn't stand a chance. Moments, only moments after Danielle cried her pleasure Nate spilled his own deep inside her. He held her tightly, resting his head on the wall and waiting for the sensitivity around his cock to stop.

In bed, Nate held onto Danielle tightly. They were once again in the spoon position with his arms wrapped around her. Covers tucked up to their waist and legs intertwined, yet Nate wasn't asleep. He was wide awake thinking about how the days were going by so fast.

"I don't want to lose you," Nate said in barely a whisper in the dark. "I don't want to let you go."

Nate closed his eyes and snuggled even closer to Danielle. He took a deep breath, forcing his body to relax, never realizing she was still awake or that she heard what he said.

* * * *

Nate bounced on the bed in the morning next to Danielle's sleeping form. He swatted her on the ass the moment he yanked the sheet away, "Get up!"

Danielle mumbled in the pillow and tried to grab the sheet. "Go away," she snapped.

Nate chuckled, giving her another smack. "I said, get up! We have a plane to catch."

Danielle sat up in the bed, but only to grab the covers and pull them over her head. "I want to sleep more."

"You can sleep later." Again he yanked the covers from her body and this time picked her up. He put her down and gave her a slight shove towards the bathroom and added, "Maybe." When she turned around and stuck her tongue out at him. Nate laughed, and added, "You keep that up and I'm going to really spank your ass."

"Yeah, yeah, yeah," she smarted back, slamming the door on him.

Forty-five minutes later Danielle walked out of the bathroom dressed in a new pair of jeans and one of the new short sleeve sweaters. Nate was sitting in a chair waiting for her dressed in jeans and a shirt as well. He had one leg crossed over the other and was tapping his fingers on the arm rest.

"Bout time," he remarked.

Danielle sat down on the bed and went to work at putting her new sneakers on. Nate stood up and tossed a small bag on the bed next to her.

"What's that for?" she asked

"That is the only bag you get to take on this trip. Pack *only* what you are going to need."

"What about Paul?"

"What about him?"

Danielle sighed. "Do you really think it's a good idea for us to just up and go out of town?"

"Well it won't hurt to get away from things." His eyes twinkled when he looked at her. "Especially work."

Danielle tossed a few personal things into the bag, but when she went to the closet to grab an outfit Nate stopped her, "But I need something to wear."

"Nope." He shook his head at her. "We are going on a shopping trip. My bag isn't any larger than yours."

"But..."

"No buts!" He handed her a jean jacket with a determined look on his face. "The only person that is allowed to call will be the hospital. For the remaining time we have together I want to take you far away."

Danielle thought she saw a small amount of regret in Nate's eyes. Whether it was from their time coming close to an end or the whole deal itself, she didn't know.

Thirty minutes later they were pulling up to a private plane. Danielle couldn't believe her luck when she stepped out of the car and followed Nate. Never in her whole life had she been on a plane, and here she was getting ready to go into one and leave the state.

As they buckled up Nate told her that he was thinking about taking her to New York but decided the he wanted to shop in Hollywood. The flight took about two hours and Danielle was shocked. Nate was ready to shop. He rented a car and drove himself down to the famous *Rodeo Drive*.

The first thing they did was look at all the fancy shops along the strip. Nate was joking about the women sticking their noses up in the air at them because of the fact they were dressed in jeans and t-shirts, not the designer clothing and dresses. Oh, how he would enjoy informing the store employees' managers that money was no object, and not giving them the time of day. Danielle looked at him as if he was crazy. Just to prove his point, he parked and dragged Danielle into one of the fancy stores.

Nate walked into *Saks Fifth Avenue.* He looked around the shop, smiling at Danielle as soon as the first clerk looked him up and down. Nate let go of Danielle's hand and walked up to a dress hanging next to the window.

"What do you think about this?" he asked her with a very ornery look and Danielle couldn't help smiling.

"Excuse me, Sir," one of the clerks said as she walked up to him, "May I help you to find a store more to your liking?"

"No." He smiled politely. "I kind of like this one."

"I see," she huffed.

"How much is it?"

The woman braced herself in a manner that spoke loud about her feelings. She wanted Nate to know that she thought she was much better than him and that there was no way in hell he could afford anything in her store.

"I'm afraid that is out of your reach."

"Is that so?" Nate placed his hands on his hips and looked at the woman. "Are you saying that you don't want to wait on me, or my girlfriend?"

"Sir, if you please…"

"No!" Nate cut her off. "Please get your manager."

The woman looked at Nate as if he had lost his mind. "Very well," she told him in a tight voice with a 'how dare you' look.

Nate winked at Danielle as he waited. Following the woman out came a man in an *Armani* suit. "May I help you?" he asked Nate in the same kind of stuffy voice.

Nate crossed his arms over his chest and gave the man a cocky smile. "Have you heard of Nathaniel Remington?"

The man put a smile on his snotty face, "My dear boy he is one of the richest men in *Forbes* magazine."

"Is that so?" Nate looked at Danielle with a huge grin on his face, "Did you hear that?"

Danielle crossed her arms over her chest. One eyebrow went up, "Don't let it go to your head."

"Oh, too late, sweetheart." He winked and added, "Now for sure we're going to have the time of our lives."

"Then, can we get out of here?" she asked him sweetly, "Snobs turn my stomach."

Nate laughed, "Yes, but before we go to the next store…" he turned back to the manager who was looking very confused. "I'm Nathaniel Remington. And I've a piece of advice before I walk out of your store, without buying anything. Work on your staff. Rich men like me tend to walk into places like this dressed as I am."

Nate took great satisfaction when all color drained from the snooty man's face and busted out laughing the moment they were back out on the street.

Danielle only shook her head at him. "Enjoyed that?" "You have no idea," he laughed, wiping the tears from his eyes.

"Neither do you," she grumbled.

Nate sobered up quickly, "What's wrong?"

Danielle stopped walking and looked at him with a somber expression, "You don't get it. That is how I get treated all the time."

Nate sighed. "Come on, Dannie. We're here to have some fun, not fight."

"You call that fun?" she cried with a frown on her face.

"As a matter of fact I do!" He rubbed his face with one hand, the other on his hip. "If I went into that shop dressed in one of my suits those women would have been kissing my ass. I was trying to make a point in there."

"The only point I saw was you acting as much of an ass as they were."

Nate groaned, but when he looked at her something hit him. Something that almost put a smile back on his face, "This isn't about what I did in that shop, is it?"

Danielle suddenly became very defensive, "I don't know what you're talking about."

"Yes you do. You're trying to start a fight with me." He grinned at her then, "Why?"

"I'm not trying to start anything with you. I just don't think you needed to act like a prick in the store."

Nate pushed his smile back. He saw the realization in her eyes and felt it as well. They only have four days left and she didn't want to leave him just as he didn't want her to leave.

"Fine," he tossed his hands up in the air, "I'll be a good boy in the stores. Happy now?"

"Yes," she told him tightly.

"Good, now can we go and spend some of my father's well earned, cut throat money?"

Danielle smiled brightly. "Now that's a deal I'll never pass up."

* * * *

Nate took Danielle into Yves Saint Laurent, & Pierre Deux. He bought her skirts and slacks with coordinating silk tops. He even included matching shoes and purses. For himself he purchased a few nice shirts, slacks and one jacket.

His favorite buy of the day for Danielle was a sexy silk ankle length nightgown and matching robe. The gown had a slit up the side and was a pale blue with thin straps and an almost see through front. If it hadn't been for the large flower pattern he would have been able to see her beautiful breasts when she wore it.

Danielle picked up cream colored silk pajama bottoms for Nate. She laughed when he told her that he was going to wear them every night to bed.

With their hands full of bags and laughing about the looks they were getting, they stopped off at a café along the road for lunch. It was nothing fancy, just some hamburgers, fries and sodas. Nate was starting to enjoy the plain and simple foods. Every time he and Dannie ate a burger it reminded him of his simple life with his mother.

Danielle thought they were done and would be heading off when they dropped their bags at the car. Nate, however, had a different idea. He tugged her into a store that she never thought, even in her wildest dreams, she would ever land a foot in. Cartier. It was one of the most famous places to buy jewelry on the strip and Danielle felt very uncomfortable standing there.

"Ah! Mr. Remington!" The gentleman behind the counter smiled brightly, "How fabulous it is to see you again!"

Danielle gave Nate a dirty look mixed with a slight grin. "It isn't how it looks!" he defended himself, "As a wedding present for my cousin I got them their wedding sets."

Danielle shook her head and went off to look at the sparkling jewelry. She saw many different styles, sizes, and stones set in everything from earrings to bracelets. However one ring at the end of the row grabbed her attention.

A large, square blue diamond with large diamonds on the side seemed to stand out from the rest. On a closer look she noticed that matching blue and white diamonds ran down halfway on the sides of the gold band.

"Ah, I see your lady has great taste." The man that was talking to Nate walked up behind the counter. He opened it, bringing out the ring. "We have only had this treasure for a few months. One of a kind," he said, taking Danielle's hand, slipping the ring onto her ring finger and smiling brightly, "That is a rare, four-caret blue diamond blue diamond. The rest of the diamonds around it, and the ones on the band total up to another caret."

"Very nice," Nate mumbled behind Danielle, looking over her shoulder at the ring on her finger.

"I bet it costs a pretty penny," Danielle remarked, taking the ring off and handing it back to the dealer.

"I have it marked at a half, but for you, Mr. Remington I will always make you a good deal."

Danielle felt as if someone just cut her air off. "Are you saying you have that at half a million?"

"Afraid so," the dealer chimed, "It is a very rare ring. Stones like that are hard to come by."

"Well not today." Nate grinned. "Just came in for the package I called for."

"Of course."

Danielle continued to look at the ring as Nate walked back with the man to finish his deal. She didn't see him look back at her a couple of times, and didn't hear him walk back up.

"Sure is something to look at," he remarked.

"Sure is," she replied softly.

Nate grinned. "Ready to go?"

Danielle snapped out of her haze to smile at him. "Yep. Where are we heading to next?"

Nate took her hand as they walked out of the shop, "Back to the plane. I want to be in Vegas before midnight."

"Vegas!" Danielle cried out, shocked. "You mean Las Vegas ?"

Nate opened the door to the car for her with a mischievous grin on his face. "That would be the one."

Danielle waited for him to start the car before she turned to him. The look on her face still showed how shocked she was. "I've never been there before."

"Then this will be something to remember." He pulled into the traffic, heading back to the plane. "The city that never sleeps. What ever you want to see or do, we'll see and do it."

Danielle laughed, "You have got to stop doing that."

"Doing what?"

"That! This!" she cried. "I don't live like this. To make me feel like this can be so real isn't right."

"You only live once, Dannie," he told her with his grin in place, "Let's live this week up to the fullest."

* * * *

The plane landed in Las Vegas around ten thirty at night. A car was waiting to pick them up and when Danielle questioned him Nate only smiled. The moment the car pulled up in front of the Luxor hotel Danielle became so shocked that she was speechless. She had seen the hotel many times on television and also dreamed about what it would be like to go there. Never really believing that she would one day be walking into the Luxor to spend a few nights.

"Call this down to earth." Nate smiled. "I could have gotten the pent house on top."

"Glad you didn't," she mumbled back as she looked around her.

Nate checked them in and they were escorted to their room on the twelfth floor by a bellhop. The man opened the door with a smile and it was then that Danielle knew there was nothing down to earth about this room.

Everything was in the Egyptian sand color. A large bathroom was to the left with a shower that could fit five. Double sinks along with a toilet and tub. The room also had a medium size living room with sofa, two chairs, TV, small fridge, and writing desk. In the center of the room sat a king size bed with four posts reaching the ceiling. Another fridge sat under a built in flat screen TV and to the sides of that were built in closets. What really had Danielle excited was the extremely large Jacuzzi in front of the big window.

Nate couldn't stop smiling as he watched Danielle look around the room, stopping at the Jacuzzi. He tipped the boy who put their bags down by the bed and quickly put the do not disturb sign on the outside of the door before closing it.

"So?" he asked cheerfully, "You like?"

Danielle touched the Jacuzzi before she looked back at Nate. "This is still too much," she told him in a breathless voice.

"Well to clear that up…" He tossed the card key on the nightstand before dropping on the bed, "…People just like you get a room just like this. When they come up to Vegas it's to splurge and have a great time. Even if it is only for three days," he winked.

"Splurge and have a good time?" she questioned him with one eyebrow raised.

"That's what I said." He closed his eyes, put his hand under his head and lay back on the bed with a sigh.

The sound of water, however, had Nate sitting up in the bed quickly. He looked over at Danielle who was yanking off her socks then kicking off her shoes. His body sprang to life quickly as he watched her strip before him facing the tub. Naked she looked over her shoulder with a grin on her face.

"Then I guess I should at least enjoy this then," she told him.

Nate found himself sitting on the bed and watching her step into the Jacuzzi, mesmerized by the sight of her beautiful body. It wasn't until the tub was full and she had turned the water off and the pumps on that he moved. With water up to her breasts and a smile on her lips, Nate was stripping. Once, he tripped on his jeans, causing Danielle to giggle at him.

Nate climbed into the tub, smiling as the jets hit his body. Danielle couldn't take her eyes off him, biting her lower lip as she watched him sinking down into the water. Neither said a word as they looked hungrily at each other. They didn't speak, they didn't have to, and their eyes said it all for them.

It was Danielle who made the move this time. Quickly moving in front of Nate, she looked him in the eyes with a very caring and surreal expression on her face. She touched his face, running a thumb over his lower lip. Nate suddenly thought that Danielle was looking at him in a manner meant to memorize him. It was moving and touching, but also depressing. He didn't want to think about how their time was running out.

Danielle kissed Nate gently. When she pulled back to look at him again Nate saw her pain clearly in her eyes. He brushed hair from her face while his other hand wrapped around her body, pressing her closer. His body was on fire with need, yet his heart was breaking for her.

Nate managed to keep his composure while she positioned herself on him. His mouth opened slightly as she sank down, taking his hard cock as deep inside her as he would go.

His eyes locked with hers as his hands held onto her hips while she moved up and down on him. Nate saw the pain, the need, and he saw her heart breaking so clearly that he couldn't do anything but hold onto her.

Water splashed over the sides and still Nate didn't move. He watched Danielle closely. Watched her pleasure spike as her body started to tighten. As her eyes closed and a frown crossed her forehead, Nate didn't move. His hands were the only thing moving. They helped her to get closer to the orgasm that was only fingertips away.

Her sucking in a breath and short jerks were the only sign Nate had that she reached what she was seeking. His own climax came, but he noticed that this time around it was different. They didn't reach the mind blowing pleasure that he was starting to expect. It was as if something in them both changed; something that he couldn't put his finger on and was afraid to think about it. Something deep in him told Nate that if he touched this crack it would all come shattering down.

Nate held her in his arms tightly, waiting. He felt the change in her, but didn't want to bring it to light. Not yet. So taking a deep breath he fought to push back all of the emotion and all of the knowledge he had and put a smile on his face.

"How about we take a nap then go out to partake of the night life?" He waited until she sat up and looked at him. Still her eyes held a touch of sadness in them that he longed to take away. "We'll go and spend some more money and try our luck at a few tables."

Danielle gave him back a tender smile, "Sounds like a plan to me."

In bed, Nate held her tightly in his arms as she slept. As much as he tried to push it away, the nagging knowledge that their time was coming to an end kept filling his mind. He didn't want to let her go. Not now. Not after he finally got her. The only trouble was he could he make her understand that they were perfect for each other?

"How do I make you see that you are everything to me?" he said softly into the night.

Chapter Eight

"Come on hard eight!" Danielle yelled, laughing.

Nate stood next to her at a craps table smiling as she rolled the dice. When the guy announced eight, he laughed. Danielle jumped up screaming, along with a few others. It was her third win at the high stakes table, giving her now at nice couple of thousand.

"You know," Nate whispered in her ear, "With all of your winnings I insist that you go shopping and spend the whole thing on yourself."

Danielle looked at him with a big smile on her face, "I think that can be easily arranged."

"Good, now roll those dice." He smiled, before kissing her on the lips. "I'm starving and there is a lobster with my name all over it."

"I swear the only thing you have on your mind is food," she remarked before she rolled the dice."

"Seven! Shooter out!"

"Damn!" Danielle cried.

"Food and you," Nate mumbled in her ear, pressing his body up close to her from behind.

Danielle made a disgusted sound as she cashed in her chips. "Oh please!" She pushed him back as she took her winnings up to the cashier's box, "So far you have gotten more sex than I think you need."

"Oh baby, one can never get enough." He gave her an ornery grin when she looked back at him, handing in her chips and waiting for the cash. "And just looking at that backside has me hungry all over again."

Danielle only shook her head at him. Joking, and her pushing him off, they walked into the restaurant that had the largest lobsters Nate had been eyeballing. They both ordered one along with the best wine in the house.

It was almost one in the morning by the time they finished their late supper. On a sigh, Danielle pushed her plate away and sat back in the over sized chair. Nate wiped his mouth, grinning at her before he also sat back.

"I think I'm going to have a couple of bottles of this wine brought up to our room." He picked the bottle up, reading the label.

"Really?" she questioned him, "And what plans do you have for the rest of the evening?"

"Well I think one bottle we'll drink," his eyes twinkled when he looked over at her, "Then maybe pour the other on your body and lick it off."

"You know one would think that after two weeks you would have had your fill," she chuckled back.

"Darling I can never get enough and the more I have, the more I want of you."

Danielle blushed as she picked her glass up. She took a tender sip before looking him in the eye again. "And what are you going to do when our time is up?"

Nate finished his own drink, keeping his eyes fixed on her, "I'm not thinking about that right now. I'm only thinking about the time we have now and how much of it I'm going to spend inside you."

Danielle lowered her eyes and took another drink of her wine before she spoke again. "I think I'm going to look for a bag in which to take my clothes home." Heat seeped into her cheeks when she looked up at him. "Can't shop more if I don't have something to put it all in."

Nate grinned. "You do that. I think I'm going to pick a few things up as well."

They agreed to meet back in the room in an hour. Danielle, however, managed to make it back before then. She knew which bag she wanted and wasted no time in buying it. In fact she was taking a hot shower when Nate came back.

He tossed his small bag on the bed with a smile and went to order a bottle of champagne from room service. By the time it came he was rock hard and ready to make what was left of this night memorable.

Stripping quickly, Nate retrieved what was in the bag. He grinned again as he looked at the cock ring and butterfly clit vibrator. He slipped the cock ring on as he walked to the bathroom. Quickly he opened the door and was greeted with heavy steam. Seeing the outline of Dannie in the shower with her back to him heightened his arousal. His cock twitched in anticipation while he placed the butterfly on the counter.

Quickly he opened the shower door and stepped in. By the time Danielle heard him he was already in. She turned around fast. Her eyes held a mixture of shock and disbelief as she looked at him in her shower.

"What are you doing?" she asked with a surprised pitch in her voice.

"I'm going to make this night last as long as I can," he told her with a hungry voice.

Nate kissed her deeply as he pressed her body up against the wall. While his tongue did a dance inside her mouth his hands slid down the sides of her body to her legs. He enjoyed the surprised sound she made when he picked her up and wrapped her legs around his waist.

Hot water beat against their bodies as tongues fought a battle for complete dominance. Danielle broke the kiss; however, the moment Nate started to slide the hard flesh between his legs inside her.

He also moaned against her neck. He closed his eyes to enjoy the feeling of her tight pussy stretching for him and from the scorching heat gripping his cock. He found that there was something different about being in the shower with hot water pouring over his body. It seemed to heighten the heat in his body, and in hers, he imagined, by ten.

When the muscles of her pussy tightened on him Nate groaned, "Oh yeah. Just like that."

Danielle also had her eyes closed and her legs and arms wrapped tightly around his body. Her mouth was open in a silent moan as he moved. Slowly pulling out only to push back in just as slowly. It was a torture she loved and hated at the same time.

"Oh, God, Nate!" she moaned as his mouth moved over her throat and his cock wound her tighter in slow movements, "I can't take this."

Nate stopped cold turkey, "Then let's see if you can handle the surprise I have waiting for you."

He turned the water off and pulled out of her sweet body. He didn't put her down but held her in his arms and walked out of the shower to sit her on the bathroom counter. With a sexy look in his eyes Nate showed her a sex toy. It was an oval shape ball on a long string with a small motor attached.

"It's called the bullet." He told her.

Danielle couldn't find any words to say. She could only watch him while he hooked the thing around her hips and legs. It fit like a pair of panties. She sucked in her breath quickly as he positioned it over her clit, pressing it in to make sure it was touching.

"Get ready for the ride of your life," he told her as he positioned the head of his cock back at her tight entrance.

Danielle groaned and her head went back the second he turned the thing on and tiny vibes touched her clit. Nate used that distraction to enter her body again with a hard thrust. The combination of the two sent Danielle over the edge. Her legs came up, knees bent under Nate's arms as she moaned her pleasure. It wasn't nearly enough for him.

Nate moved his hips hard and fast. He moaned with each hard push back inside her, for that also gave him a slight vibe from the butterfly.

"Oh shit!" Danielle suddenly cried.

Her orgasm hit her fast and hard, causing her to almost crawl up on Nate. He held her tight, but also continued to move his hips hard, forcing her to ride out the pleasure. The moment she came down he picked her back up and walked out of the bathroom. He walked to the bed where he sat down.

"Turn around," he told her in a rough voice.

Danielle was in such a daze from the butterfly keeping her on the edge, that she found herself doing as he said before she even thought about what he was doing. By the time she sat back down on his lap she was facing away from him, and Nate had his cock imbedded deeply.

Danielle rested her head on his shoulder as his hands cupped her breasts. Her hands touched his as his legs went to work at moving them.

"Move," he told her in her ear, "Move just like this."

Danielle bounced on Nate quickly just like he showed her. Her crying out in ecstasy almost had Nate coming, but he managed to push it back. He was saving his orgasm for the last. He wanted to make damn sure that when she slept tonight nothing crossed her mind but him.

Her hands tightened over his and her moaning mixed with crying had Nate also moaning. Her whole body tightened up, making him think about the first time he loved her. The first time he entered her body. She was so tight, so perfect that he knew he couldn't let her go. Not now, not after all they shared in the past two weeks.

"Nate!" Danielle screamed.

Nate groaned loudly when she came. Her whole body tightened so hard on his cock that he couldn't keep moving.

"God I love it when your body tightens up like that," he told her softly as his hands fondled her breasts.

Danielle was breathing so hard that she thought she was going to pass out from it. "I can't take any more."

"Yes you can." Nate stood up, pulling out of her. His whole cock was so sensitive that just the right amount of pressure would tip him over the edge.

He stood Danielle on her feet, bending her over and coming up behind. His arm snaked around to the vibrator, turning it up a notch. He smiled when he heard her combination of groaning and moaning.

Carefully he parted the cheeks of her ass, looking at the small puckered ring that he'd had only once. He wanted it again. Wanted to brand her one more time to him in every way he could. Wanted Danielle to remember him no matter what part of her body was touched.

The sun had started to rise when Nate made his choice. Holding her tightly and turning the vibrator up as high as it would go, he pushed the head of his cock at the tiny ring. Danielle stiffened up, but Nate didn't back down. He wanted this one more time and nothing she said or did was going to make him stop.

"Nate," she moaned, "Please, don't!"

"Too late," he hissed back.

Her body started to shake with pleasure and he managed to use his way inside her with little force. He'd guessed she was more than ready for this new invasion from him. The moment his plum sized head was inside her he was home free. Closing his eyes, Nate gave up his fight for control. He moved fast, moaning with each stroke inside as he felt the vibrations from her butterfly.

"I'm so close, Dannie," he moaned in her ear as he kissed and licked the lobe, "So fucking close I need you to come. I need to hear you scream as I give you intense pleasure. I want to hear you cry out from what I alone give you."

Nate moved his hand down between her legs as his hips continued to pound into her ass. He shoved two fingers deep inside her pussy. It was enough. Danielle screamed in pleasure and Nate lost his battle. He came hard and heavy deep inside her ass, holding her as tightly to him as he could.

"Don't leave, Dannie," he said into her hair as he rubbed his face in the silky strands, "Don't leave me."

Nate waited for a response but heard none. When he pulled out of her body to look at her, Danielle was out cold. With a caring smile on his face, Nate placed her in the bed and cleaned them both up. The clock on the nightstand next to the bed read five in the morning when he crawled in next to her and fell into a deep sleep.

* * * *

Nate was dreaming that his cell phone was vibrating. Someone was trying to get in touch with him, but he was too far away to reach. At least he thought he was dreaming it. Slowly he opened his eyes and turned his head to the nightstand. He was sleeping on his stomach, as was Danielle. His arm and half of his body seemed to be over hers, and she still seemed to be sleeping deeply. The clock read, two in the afternoon. And yes, his cell was vibrating on the nightstand.

With a deep groan he moved away from Danielle and snatched his phone. The ID told him it was his office and the only reason they would be calling was if this was something about life or death. Anything else could get the caller fired on the spot.

Rolling over onto his back, and careful to not wake Dannie, he answered with a tight, "Yes."

"I'm sorry to disturb you." It was his secretary, Nancy. "But the hospital called. Mr. Hughes was taken into emergency surgery an hour ago."

Nate sat up in bed. "Is everything all right, Nancy?"

"Yes Sir." He could hear the happiness in her voice. "He went in for a sudden liver transplant. A donor was found!"

"That's great!" Nate looked at the sleeping form of Dannie, smiling at how she slept. The sheet barely covered her and he found he wanted her again right this minute. "Call the pilot. Have him get the plan ready to fly us home. Tell him to be ready in about an hour."

Nate hung the phone up then tossed it back to the night stand. He scooted back into the bed, hugging up to her. Rubbing his hand up and down her back he worked at waking her up gently. Nate knew that they had a long night and that both needed more sleep. He also knew that she would be very sore, but if he didn't wake her up and get her back home before Paul came out of surgery he was going to be a dead man.

"Wake up, sleeping beauty," he said before he kissed her bare back, pulling the sheet away, "Time to get up."

Danielle groaned, "Go away."

"We need to get up," he told her, "I have some great news for you."

"You brought me breakfast?" she asked, looking for the covers.

"It's Paul."

The name seemed to snap Danielle wide awake. She flipped over to her sore ass, looking at Nate with fright in her eyes, "What's wrong?"

"Nothing bad," he told her, kissing her lightly on her lips, "He went into surgery. They found him a liver and are doing the transplant right now."

Tears formed in her eyes as she looked at Nate as all of the information sank in. Out of no where she flung herself into his arms, crying happy tears. Nate held her, closing his own eyes and taking a deep breath.

"If you want to be on the plane heading home in an hour then you had better get that fine ass of yours in the shower." She looked at him with a teary smile on her face, "Before I decide to have my way with you again."

It was an hour and ten minutes later that they pulled up to the plane. Danielle was smiling brightly as she handed her bag off and climbed inside. She couldn't believe that finally, after all this time; her brother was getting the liver he needed. Finally he was going to be healthy again.

Nate had the car waiting for them the moment they landed. He also called the hospital and was told everything went fine. Paul was just coming out of surgery and was being taken to recovery. So far his body wasn't rejecting the liver.

Danielle was so excited to see her brother that she barely managed to wait for the car to stop before she was out of it. Nate chuckled at her as she ran to the elevator. Her smile, however dropped when she came face to face with her parents waiting in the family waiting room for news of Paul.

"Well, well, well," Robert snarled, "The caring daughter makes an appearance from her vacation to check in on her brother."

Nate saw the sudden change in Danielle. For the past few weeks he had her relaxed and enjoying life, coming back home to her family put her right back in the place where he wanted to remove her.

"Nate, will you please give us a few moments," she said, keeping her eyes on her father, "I would like to have a few words with my father."

"Dannie, I don't think…" he started to say.

She turned around, showing him strength that he never saw before, "Please. I need to do this alone."

Nate nodded his head after a few moments. "If you need me, I'll be at the nurse's desk."

"Well, isn't that something," Robert smarted off, "Your own knight in shinning armor."

"Cut the shit!" Danielle hissed at him, "I am so sick of it!"

"You watch your tongue, girl!"

"Or what?" Danielle charged up to him. "You going to hit me again? Beat your love into me and make me feel like I'm dirt beneath your feet?" A tear suddenly slipped out of her eye as she looked up at the man from whom she'd wanted nothing more than love. "I used to cry to Paul every night for you. I wanted nothing but one small ounce of love from you. All I got was your hate."

"Dannie, please," Marie put in, "That isn't true."

"Paul is my brother but he loved me like a father should his daughter. He's more man than you can ever be."

"And you show your respect to this family by whoring after that man?" Robert accused. "You would let him use you then toss you aside like all the other girls?"

Danielle walked away from him, running her hands into her hair and pushing back the tears of pain. "I took care of my brother," she turned back around, "I did what you wanted. We all did what you wanted."

Robert watched her pull out a large envelope from her purse. She tossed it to the table, "What's this?" he asked.

"My last obligation to this family. I have been carrying it around for two weeks." She watched him open it and pull out the papers. "Everything you and mom own is paid for. Even the house. That's the deed. You're now debt free." She waited for him to look up at her with disbelief in his eyes. "I'm also moving out. All of my things will be out by tomorrow night."

Danielle turned and walked out of the room. She found Nate looking over some files. He was so deep in thought that he never heard her walking up. When he did finally notice her Nate smiled brightly.

"Looks as if everything is going great for your brother."

"Can we get out of here?"

Nate picked up right off that something wasn't right with Dannie. Seemed that the moment she came face to face with her father she changed. It was a sight that he didn't like and something he didn't know how to fix.

"Sure."

Danielle started to walk off but stopped. Her head was down in deep thought before she looked back up at him. "Better yet, how about if I meet you later on tonight. There are a few things I want to take care of now."

Nate's heart started to pound in his chest, "Okay. Why don't you take the car and I can get caught up on a few things around here?"

Danielle nodded her head and walked away. Nate just stood there. He could feel the loss starting and was powerless to prevent any of it. He only had a deal to spend two weeks with her. That deal was coming to an end and there wasn't one damn thing that crossed his mind to put a halt on it.

* * * *

Danielle had the driver drop her off at her parent's home. She told him that he could go back to Nate and let Nate know she would meet him at his home later tonight. Pushing all of her emotions aside, Danielle walked into the house and headed straight for her room. She pulled out all of her suitcases and bags and began working hard at packing as much of her things as she could.

By the time she was done, Danielle had four suitcases, three bags, and three boxes full of her stuff. She dragged everything out to the front where she waited for a cab she had called. An hour later she was unpacking her clothes in the hotel room she rented for the week. Danielle thought that would give her enough time to figure out what she was going to do when the last night with Nate came around.

Close to two, Danielle called another cab and headed back to Nate's home. Nate came out of the house and Danielle found herself walking into his arms. She closed her eyes as his arms wrapped around her frame. She tried to store each and every one of these moments into her memory for later.

"Come on," he told her, resting his chin on the top of her head, "I have some dinner waiting for you."

With his arm still around her, Nate walked Danielle back inside his home. He walked her to the kitchen where he sat her down at the table. For most of the night they talked about their high school years, is being in the most popular group and her being the loner in school. They even recalled the fight she got into with one of his old girlfriends. Nate then went on to explain how he never knew what happened to her then. One day she was no longer in his PE class. Danielle told him that to keep peace she was put into a different class, but that they did have History together.

After helping with dishes both decided to take a bath together. Nate found that he only wanted to hold her. He wanted to wrap his arms around her body and never let go. It seemed that the two of them were suffering; they didn't want their time together to come to an end. They both felt the pain of the coming separation, but it wasn't anything they could talk about.

So for the longest time Nate lay in bed, in a spoon position, with Danielle held tightly in his arms until sleep finally gripped them both.

Chapter Nine

Nate groaned in his sleep. He was dreaming about hot lips rubbing over the head of his cock and a wet tongue sliding down the underside. He moaned as the tongue in his dream slid back up to the head, swirling around the tiny hole. Only when a mouth closed around the head and sank down the base did Nate figure out that this wasn't a dream.

His eyes snapped open as he sucked in his breath and looked down his body. Dannie was between his legs, sucking on his cock in such a tender, loving manner that it tore at his heart.

Up and down her head bobbed over him, drawing Nate closer to the completion that he found only Dannie could give him.

"Oh man!" Nate hissed as she sucked him harder. He rose up on his elbows and bent his knees slightly. The sight of her hair covering the action and the sight of her head going up and down increased his desire. There was nothing as beautiful as having a woman that grabbed his heart the way Dannie did, loving him in the manner that she was doing right now. "God I have died and gone to heaven."

Danielle made a popping sound the moment she released his cock. Her tongue snaked out and licked at his flat stomach as she moved her body upward, "Then let's see if I can finish you off."

Danielle pushed Nate down on his back. His hands went up to her waist as she positioned herself over him. He looked up, watching her as she pulled her nightgown up over her head and tossed it to the side.

He said nothing as she took hold of his cock, rubbing it over the wet slit of her pussy. Her mouth opened as she kept her eyes locked with his. Slowly Danielle took him deep inside her body, gripping him tightly as only a lover would do.

Nate felt the change in her. He felt the way she was trying to shut herself off to the world. Felt her going back to the old shell of a woman. And there wasn't a damn thing he could do.

Her hips moved slowly, but steady. Nate knew that she was working hard at making this last, just as he would if he had thought about waking her in the middle of the night. However she was making it a task he found very difficult to do. Her body gripped him so perfectly that he felt it deep within his soul.

Nate moved his hands up to her breasts, cupping the mounds firmly. He watched with pleasure as her mouth opened and her head went back on a sigh. He saw it in her eyes, just before they closed; saw how much she loved for him to touch her just like this.

Nate bucked his hips under her, picking up the tempo. Danielle followed his lead and leaned forward with her hands on his chest. Her hips began to move harder, faster and it took everything in Nate not to take over. The urge to pound her onto him was overwhelming.

"God, Dannie," Nate moaned out in a tension filled voice.

Nate closed his eyes and turned his head, kissing her arm. He was so close that it was almost a painful thing. Yet, when he opened his eyes Nate saw something that really tore at him. Tears were falling from Danielle's closed eyes while she continued to ride him gently.

Nate sat up suddenly, wrapping his arms around her body. Danielle continued to move her hips but she also cried on his shoulder. Out of no where her head went back, mouth open with a silent moan, and a small orgasm rushed into her. Nate felt it, but it didn't seem to do anything for him. So he moved his arms down and hooked her legs under them. Quickly, and with hard, powerful movements he pounded her onto him.

He was so fast and so hard that Danielle had to hold onto his shoulders tightly. Whimpering came from Danielle's lips that only fueled Nate further. He slammed her as fast and as hard as he could, feeling his balls tighten with the need for release.

On a groan, Nate kissed her deeply. Pleasure erupted hot and thick deep inside him. Danielle was whimpering as she ground her hips down onto Nate. He tasted salty tears while he kissed her face, waiting for the spasms to stop.

Nate was surprised to find himself still hard inside her. After the sweet pleasure, and seeing the pain in Dannie's eyes, Nate was shocked to feel the need to have her again.

He shifted them both, laying Danielle under him gently. Tenderness filled his whole body as he brushed hair from her face. More tears fell from her eyes while Nate looked down at her.

"God, you are so beautiful," he told her in a soft, emotion-filled voice.

Danielle began to cry even more as she pulled him down to her, wrapping her legs and arms tightly around him. Nate buried his face into her neck and closed his eyes tightly. She ground her hips under him, causing Nate to lose his guilt about wanting her again so soon.

Moving his head in order to look at her again, Nate moved his hips slowly. He loved her gently and softly. His lips pecked, and then nipped on her own. Their tongues darted out to tease one another, and still tears fell from Danielle's eyes.

When her arms pulled Nate back down, he went. He buried his face into her soft shoulder as he buried his cock in and out of her body. Danielle's moans of pleasure were mixed with her soft crying. Nate's orgasm poured out of him as he wrapped his arms tightly around her body. Held her while his cock spasmed its release and her body contracted around it. It was a moment that no matter how hard he might try, Nate would never forget.

For the longest time Nate stayed awake holding Dannie tightly in his arms. They were in the spoon position with his arms tightly wrapped around her. His legs were also intertwined with hers and the covers were kicked down to the end. The clock on the nightstand told him it was two in the morning, and her breathing told him that she was deep asleep.

"Oh, Dannie," he sighed to himself, "What are we going to do?"

The phone woke Nate up at six in the morning. He jumped with the first ring and by the second he rolled away from Dannie to answer it.

"This better be important," he hissed into the phone.

"I'm sorry to bother you at home, Mr. Remington," his secretary Nancy said in the phone, "but we have a problem here that needs your immediate attention."

Nate sighed heavily as he swung his legs over the side of the bed, "What is it?"

"It's the Bental deal," Nancy went on. "Your lawyer has found a crack in the paper work and fears that the board will use it. He wanted me to call you, Sir, and have you come in right away."

Nate rubbed his hand over his face. "Let them know I'll be in within an hour."

He hung the phone up and looked over his shoulder at Dannie. He was partially surprised to find her still asleep. He was also pissed that he had to go into the office right this minute. Getting out of bed and walking to the bathroom, Nate kept going over and over in his mind the things he wanted to say to Dannie tonight.

Thirty minutes later he was dressed in one of his designer suits with the present he had for Dannie in his pocket. He was planning on giving it to her tonight at dinner along with asking her to stay with him. With a smile on his face he walked over to the bed and bent down, giving her a light kiss on the cheek.

With the front door closed behind Nate, Danielle's eyes snapped open. She had heard all that he said on the phone and decided to use his going into the office to pack her things up. With a regretful heart she slipped out of the bed and into the bathroom. For at least twenty minutes she stood under the hot water, crying. Her heart was breaking over her having to leave tonight and there wasn't a thing she could do about it.

By noon Danielle had everything that Nate bought her packed up. A cab she had called was out front, loading up everything but the one bag she had in her hand. Pushing back tears that threatened to fall again she walked around Nate's home one more time. She smiled in the living room as she remembered the movie night and how that ended.

Turning off the last light, Danielle walked out of house. She left the key that Nate had given her on the small table by the front door. Not once did she look back as the cab pulled away.

* * * *

Marie Hughes walked into her daughter's bedroom and almost screamed when she saw Danielle sitting in the window seat with all the lights turned off. She could tell by the way Dannie was sitting with her head back on the window and her legs drawn up that she was very upset.

"Dannie?" Marie called out gently, "What are you doing here?"

"I'm saying good-bye to my old life," she answered back with a dead, depressed voice.

Marie walked over to the window seat, sitting down across from her daughter. Gently she took hold of her chin, forcing Dannie to look at her. "There isn't much that I can say to you that will help to take away the pain you're feeling. Seems that I haven't been the kind of mother that you needed."

Danielle smiled which only brought a fresh set of tears falling. Marie pulled her daughter into her arms, holding her like she used to when she was young.

For the longest time, Danielle cried in her mother's arms like a little girl. She cried for her broken heart, for the years of having no life, and she cried for what she was about to do. She couldn't remember the last time her mother had held her and let her cry.

At four, Danielle stood on the front steps with her mother. She was holding her hand, waiting for the cab she'd called. The cab that was going to take her to Nate's office

"Are you sure about this?" Marie asked when the yellow cab pulled up. "Once you take this step you can't go back."

"I know." Danielle took a deep breath, giving her mother's hand a tight squeeze. "But it has to be done."

Marie pushed back her own set of tears as she looked at Dannie. "You will at least call me?"

Danielle smiled. "At least every night."

"And you will go see Paul before…"

"As soon as I'm finished, I will."

Marie nodded her head. "Then you go do what you think you need to do."

* * * *

Nate paced his office with a folder open in one hand and a phone in the other. His anger was rising as the deal he had been working on for almost a year was in danger of crumbling. The merger was set, and then the board found a savior. It was not the best of news, and the situation was taking his whole team working together in order to fix it.

Glancing at his watch again, Nate swore under his breath. He wanted to be out of the office and in a nice restaurant with Dannie, not spending it trying to save something his father started.

"Is this a bad time?"

Nate stopped his pacing and smiled. Dannie stood by the door and she was a sight for his sore eyes. He'd never thought to see anything as good as Dannie standing there. "I'll call you back," Nate spoke into the phone as he hung it up.

"It's never a bad time for you." He grinned and said, "This damn deal might fall through and it's fifty million. Guess we're going to have to do dinner another night."

Danielle closed the door behind her and hung her head. Her sigh had Nate's heart dropping to his stomach. His gut told him that something was not right here; something that he wasn't going to like one bit.

"Dannie?" he asked her in a cautious manner, "Is everything alright?"

Danielle took a deep breath. She kept her eyes averted from him. It was another thing that had Nate very nervous, "I don't know how to say this...so I'm just going to be blunt." She looked up at him and right off, Nate saw the tears that threatened to fall. "I have to go."

Nate frowned, "Go? What do you mean?"

One tear slipped. "I have to leave before things start to become too comfortable for me." She brushed the tear away and put her hand up to stop him before he could speak. "It's time for me to stand on my own two feet. You have given me the chance to do that and I intend to." More tears fell from her eyes as she looked at him and saw the pain in his own eyes. "I'm so sorry, Nate. We both knew that this was going to happen. But we're heading toward something that neither one of us is ready for. I don't fit into your world, so I need to get out before it brings you down as well."

"You fit more than you know," he told her softly, feeling his own pain surface.

Danielle shook her head, "I can't do this," she told him as she cried softly. "We had a good time. Great in fact, but you know what they say about things that are great. They must come to an end."

"Dannie, I don't..." Nate was interrupted by his phone ringing, and his secretary buzzing in at the same time.

Danielle brushed more of her tears away as Nate walked to his intercom, "What is it Nancy?"

"They're here, Sir."

Danielle took a deep breath, "You need to get back to work and I need to get out of here."

Nate ran his hands through his hair in a frustrated motion, "I don't want you to get out of here. I want to talk about this."

"I'm sorry, Sir." Nancy came walking into the office suddenly. "Mr. Carter has arrived and has informed us that if you don't come at once he is pulling everything."

Danielle met Nate's eyes. Unspoken words went back and forth as his secretary started grabbing folders and other things.

"Sir, please!"

Nate shook his head and followed his secretary. At the door he stopped, where Danielle was still standing. His hand reached out, touching her cheek and bringing her close. His lips came down, touching hers softly. Resting his forehead against hers, Nate lingered as long as he could before he spoke. "If you need me for anything, you call me."

Danielle nodded her head yes and said nothing as he placed a box in her hand and another kiss to her forehead before he walked out of the office.

Only when the door closed behind him, did Danielle release the breath she didn't realize she was holding. She closed her eyes and let the tears fall freely. Sniffing them back she raised her chin and walked out of the office, thanking God the lobby was empty.

Outside Danielle didn't fight the tears any longer. She stood on the sidewalk looking at nothing letting her pain loose. It took her a few moments before she noticed that she was holding something that Nate had put in her hand.

Crying, Danielle opened the box to find a gold Rolex watch. She smiled through her tears, noticing the inscription on the back of the watch.

Our time is priceless, just as you are. Let's never let it run out.

Danielle slipped the watch on and turned around, looking up at the building. She couldn't see a thing, but something told her that Nate was watching her; watching her walk right out of his life.

"Good-bye," she said softly to herself.

Nate *was* watching. He stood at the board room window as Danielle stepped into a cab, carrying her away from him—out of his life. All he did was stand there like an ass, letting her go. Even the arguing that was going on couldn't seem to pull him away from the scene below. Pride prevented him from running down there and stopping her. His heart, however, was screaming out in pain. The hurt that was racing within him had Nate wanting to toss everything aside to bring back the woman he loved more than all his money. He never wanted this; never wanted the power and money if he couldn't have someone to share it with.

Now, Nate thought, now he understood why his mother left. It had nothing to do with loving his father. It had to do with her fitting into his life. James Remington cared more for his fortune than he did for his family. It was the one and only lesson Nate's mother taught him. If and when the day came that he was fortunate enough to find his true love then he was to do everything to keep it.

"Don't piss it away like your father did," his mother told him on her death bed. "When you find that girl you hold onto her with your life. There aren't any second chances in the game of love. Don't be a lonely old man with more money than brains."

"Mr. Remington!"

Nate turned away from the window, squared his shoulders to deal with the irate men at the meeting.

* * * *

Danielle went back to her hotel room. She drew herself a hot bath where she ended up sitting and crying. With all the things she had to do in her life, this was the hardest. To walk away from him knowing that she would never see his face again or feel his touch was killing her soul. But how could she stay? How could she stay there being so close knowing that he would never love her the way she loved him.

After soaking until the water was cold, Danielle got out and dressed in a pair of her old jeans and a big baggy sweater. She slipped on her sneakers, deciding it was time to go and check on Paul. On the way to the hospital she made one small stop, knowing that this was going to rock her brother's world.

Paul was sleeping by the time she got there and Danielle found a nurse that let her sit in the room with him. She noticed right off that his skin color was so good that he didn't have that look of a man who had been sick for so long.

"He's been asking about you."

Danielle jumped and turned to find her father sitting in the dark watching Paul with a smile on his face. The look on his face was one that Danielle hadn't seen in a very long time.

"What are you doing here?" she asked him in a whisper.

"Watching my boy sleep." He sleeps so much better now. The new liver is working great."

Danielle could only stare at her father in disbelief. He was acting so much like the man he used to be and it did nothing but piss her off. How could he sit there and act as if nothing happened between the two of them. That nothing bad was between them.

Danielle watched her father with a frown in place as he stood up from his chair, "I think I'm going to head home and let your mother know that you're here with him." He smiled, rubbing his hands together. "And that soon all of us will be home again as a family should be."

Danielle could only shake her head as her hand went up to her forehead. She took a deep breath, trying to get rid of the sudden tension that always seemed to grip her when her father was around.

Taking a seat in the large chair at the foot of the bed, Danielle pulled a cover over her legs and watched her brother sleep. She went over and over in her mind the things that she was going to say to Paul. She also went over the things that she wasn't going to tell him.

Chapter Ten

"Well I must say that is the most pathetic scene I've ever laid eyes on."

Danielle's head snapped up from her drawn up legs. She smiled when she saw her brother grinning at her. "You're awake!"

"And hurting like hell, I might add," he complained.

Danielle got out of the chair to sit next to her brother on the bed. She smiled as happy tears fell from her eyes. "You look damn good."

Paul smiled, but it was a tired smile. "And I do feel better. Amazing how a new body part can fix you right up."

Danielle laughed but it quickly turned into a fresh onset of crying. Even though Paul was still weak and very tired he pulled his sister down, hugging her as tightly as he could.

"To do what you did took more guts than anyone knows," he told her softly. "And to have to bear all of my health problems as you did is unforgivable."

Danielle raised her head and laughed suddenly. She stood up from the bed, walking over to the window as she cleaned her face up as best she could with her hands. "If I had to, I would do it all over again."

"He's a man you've wanted since school."

Danielle turned around quickly to look at her brother. She frowned. "How did you know?"

"Dad." Paul grimaced as he moved in the bed. "Seems the old fart couldn't wait to inform me of what you had done."

"The whore of a daughter," she replied in a dead voice. "Selling her body to pay a bill."

"Oh I think you're more like my savior." Paul hit the button on the bed that raised the head up slightly. "I don't think less of you for going out and living for a change."

"Is this living?" She leaned back on the window, crossing her arms over her chest. "All I've ever known has been a life wrapped around you. I'm so miserable that I feel like I'm going to suffocate."

"So fix it."

Danielle looked hard at her brother. Being sick for so long his cheerful brown eyes were now dull. The soft brown of his hair even looked dull from the sickness. Paul stood at five eleven. He was built like a football player but never acted like one. Their father wanted Paul to go pro. Had even called scouts to come and watch Paul in games. The day they found out Paul's liver was failing almost killed Robert. It was then that Paul knew his father was trying to live the football dream through his son.

The sickness though gave Paul a new outlook on life. His eyes opened up more to how Robert treated Danielle. He also noticed how lonely his sister really was. Being five years older than her he was able to watch her closer. High school years were supposed to be something enjoyable for a girl, yet Robert managed to make it hell.

Paul used to get into many arguments with his father about letting Dannie be a kid instead of a provider. Some of what Paul did helped her, but when he had to go into the hospital and stay was when hell came to his sister. With no one there to protect her or stand up for her, Robert walked over her even more.

He only knew about a few of the things that Dannie wanted in her life, and that was when he pried it out of her. One of those things had always been Nate Remington.

"I can't fix something that was never meant to be," she told him.

"You'll never know what was meant or not meant to be until you go and try to take a chance," Paul told her, looking at his sister closely.

Danielle looked at Paul hard before she rubbed her face, brushing her hair from her eyes. Taking a deep breath and rubbing her shoulders she began to pace the tiny room. "It's not that simple."

"Oh bullshit, Dannie!" Paul hissed in pain then cursed himself for getting so excited.

"Paul, if you don't calm down they're going to kick me out," Dannie told him sternly, sitting down on the bed.

Paul took hold of her wrist, breathing hard. "You've lived far too long in everyone's shadow. It is time for you to do what you want. Stop doing what he tells you to do."

Dannie brushed hair from her brother's eyes and smiled. "That's just what I am planning on doing." She took another deep breath, dropping her eyes and thinking about how she was going to word this. "I didn't just come here to see how you were doing. I came here to tell you good-bye."

Paul frowned, not understanding. "Good-bye? What do you mean?"

Danielle pulled out an envelope from her back pocket and handed it to Paul.

He looked down at it, then back up at her. "What's this?"

"I want you to take this and get away from him. I want you to start a new life of your own," she told him as a fresh batch of tears fell. "I want you to live your life, just as you're telling me to live mine."

"And what are you going to do?"

Danielle closed her eyes while the tears poured out of them. She took another deep breath before they opened and looked at Paul again. "I'm going to take what is left of my heart and leave. It's time for me to stand on my own two feet and not look back at the past mistakes."

"Dannie…"

Danielle stood up, cutting her brother off. "I can't stay here any longer, Paul. I can't live in that house and act like nothing has happened, or that there isn't any bad blood between us. I can't walk down the street looking over my shoulder and wondering if he's going to show up. Then pray he does, only to get hurt when he doesn't."

"You're running off to hide like a wounded animal," he told her softly.

"Then when my wounds heal they'll stay healed."

"Ah, you're awake." A nurse walked in with a smile on her face. "Time for me to check your incision."

"I need to go. Need to get my things packed and shipped out." Danielle grabbed her bag and walked to the door.

"Dannie," Paul called out. She stopped. "You will at least let me know where you settle?"

Danielle looked over her shoulder and grinned. "Only if you promise to not let him touch anything that I just gave you."

"Deal," he told her with his own caring smile.

By midnight Danielle was on a plane. She sat in the window seat watching the city life that she used to know slowly disappear. As much as she wanted to cry over the loss of not only her family but the one love of her life, she couldn't. Danielle refused to shed one more tear over her past and what could never be in her life. Only when she could see nothing more of the city did she sit back in her seat and let the tension in her body out.

* * * *

Nate stood outside his home on the balcony. He leaned on the railing with a drink of scotch in his hand. He was numb from the inside out. So numb that not even his father's best scotch could touch it. Sitting on the table next to the bottle was a small velvet box—a gift that was waiting for him when he got home— a gift that Nate wouldn't be able to give Dannie.

"Sir?"

Nate took a drink before he turned. "Yes, Jay."

Jay was his butler, and gone the whole time Danielle was here. Nate didn't want to share her with anyone, and he made sure he didn't have to. "She left the city. A midnight flight. That's all I could find."

Nate finished his drink in one large gulp. "Thank you, Jay."

"Will you need anything else?"

"No, Jay," Nate answered with a dead voice. "Nothing else will do."

* * * *

Four months later…

"No, Mike, you're not hearing me," Nate hissed into the phone as he stood up behind his desk. "I want to sell that and I want it done by the end of the week. I don't give a damn if my father bought it years ago. It means shit to me!"

"Sir! You can't go in there. Sir!"

Nate frowned as he heard Nancy yelling at someone next to his office door.

"This will be real quick," a man's voice said as the door opened. Paul Hughes rushed past Nancy, who was still trying to block him from entering Nate's office. "We need to talk. Now!"

"Mike, I'm going to have to call you back." Nate hung the phone up and looked at Dannie's irate brother. "I can take it from here, Nancy."

"Yes, Sir," she replied in a tight voice, glaring at Paul.

"Been a long time," Nate said. "Glad to see that you're out and about."

"Cut the shit, Nate." Paul slammed the door closed, crossing his arms over his chest. "I came here so you can tell me how long this shit is going to last."

"Excuse me?" Nate frowned, placing his hands on his hips in an authoritative manner.

Paul rushed up to the desk where he leaned forward, hands braced flat towards Nate, "I want to know how much longer my sister has to suffer and be alone."

Nate rubbed his face before he walked around his desk. "She left me." He looked at Paul, showing him how angry he was every time he thought about it. "Dannie had everything packed and her decision made before she came to say good-bye to me. So if she is suffering then it's her fault, not mine."

"Do you ever listen to yourself?" Paul stood back up, turning so he was still facing Nate. "From all the things you used to tell us back in high school about your old man, all the shit he did and how miserable he was, now you want to be just like him."

"I'm nothing like him!" Nate hissed back.

"You sure as hell could have fooled me." Paul plopped down in one of the chairs with a sigh. "Look. I'm not here to judge you, or tell you how to run your life. I'm here because my

114

baby sister has only me to look after her. Our father is a real bastard when it comes to her. He's always treated Dannie as if she wasn't his. He treats strangers with more feeling. When I made sure to let him know I didn't like how he treated her it left a bad taste in his mouth, but he hasn't changed how he feels about her. She deserves more than just one ounce of happiness in her life and for what ever reason her happiness depends on you."

"Then why did she leave?" Nate sighed back, feeling defeated. He looked at Paul with the same defeated expression on his face that was in his voice. "I wanted to give her the world."

"What about your heart?" Paul asked very softly, "Are you prepared to give that to her, too?"

Nate dug into his pocket and pulled out a small box. He tossed it to Paul. "Here's your answer."

Paul didn't open the box. He found that he didn't have to. Just holding it Paul knew exactly how Nate felt about his sister.

"Well I guess I'm going to ask you the same thing I asked her." Paul tossed the box back to Nate and looked the man in the eye. "What are you going to do about it now?"

Nate stuffed the box back into his pocket. His face was a mask of all seriousness as he looked back at Paul. "Nothing."

Paul grinned as he chuckled. "You're such a chicken shit."

Nate groaned, put his face into his hands suddenly and slumped into the chair next to Paul. "What the hell am I going to do?"

Paul slapped him on the back. "Lucky for you that I'm here to bail your rich ass out."

"This wouldn't be the same advice you gave Dannie before she left, is it?" He looked at Paul with one raised brow. When Paul only smiled back and bit his lower lip, Nate stood back up. "No thanks."

"Oh, come on!" Paul jumped up, following Nate to the door. "Are you going to tell me that you have a better plan? Because so far you aren't doing that great on your own."

"Have you ever thought that you might not know your sister as well as you think?" Nate challenged back. "I mean she was the one who left here."

Paul sighed. "Will you stop being an ass and look at what's in front of you. She's had a thing for you since the first time she saw you, since high school for Christ sakes. You were just too damn busy living the good life to take notice."

"That's bullshit and you know it!" Nate yelled. "I've wanted your sister from the first day I saw her. No one could get close to her in school."

"And I so love the way you got close to her now," Paul remarked dryly.

"If you're looking for me to apologize to you then you might have a better chance getting ice water in hell." The look that Nate gave Paul should have sent warning bells off, but didn't.

"And here I was starting to think you didn't give a damn," Paul grinned.

Nate could only stare at him as if he'd lost his mind. He watched with a frown in place as Paul walked back to the door.

"Meet you at your plane, say six."

"For what?" Nate asked.

Paul turned around with a big smile on his face. "You're going to make this all right with my sister, even if I have to drag your ass all the way there."

Paul walked out of the office, shutting the door with a smile on his face. He walked up to Nancy 's desk, giving her a wink.

"How did it go?" she asked.

"Couldn't have gone better. Thanks for the heads up."

Nancy smiled. "I worked for his father, remember? I don't want him to end up like old man Remington. A man without a heart is nothing more than a cold hearted bastard."

"You couldn't have said it better."

"I'll have the plane prepared and the pilot will know about the destination."

"When this is all over, I'm going to make sure he gives you a raise." Paul picked up her hand, kissing it with a grin.

"You can call it all even if you only take my granddaughter out on a date," she smiled back.

Paul groaned, "You drive a hard bargain."

Nancy stood up with some files. She smiled at Paul, touching his chin in a playful manner. "I do work for the best."

"That you do." He smiled, shaking his head as he dug into his pocket for his cell. Catching the elevator Paul called Danielle, "Hey girl, what's shaking?"

"Paul! What are you doing?"

Paul smiled as he stepped off the elevator and left the building. "I'm checking up on you. Thought I would call and see if you can squeeze me in for a visit."

"You're going to come all the way out here to see me?" The shock was apparent in her voice.

"Sure, why not," he told her cheerfully, "I hear it's the city that never sleeps."

"Sure," she stuttered out, "But I'm working all this week. Not sure when or if I'll be much company."

"Oh don't worry about me too much," he told her with a bright sounding voice, "You just leave the key under the pot and I'll let myself in. You'll find me waiting tonight to see you."

"Tonight!" she cried, "You're coming out tonight?"

"Why put off till tomorrow what can be done tonight?" He laughed into the phone, "And I'm due for a vacation. Besides, maybe I miss you." After a long pause, Paul went on, "So hey. I'm catching a flight around six, so leave me the key and I'll show myself in. It will be a vacation to remember."

Danielle laughed over the phone, "Okay. The big fern with the blue pot. Now I hate to cut this short, but I need to go."

"See you in a few hours then."

"Bye Paul."

Paul hung up his phone the same moment that a cab pulled up. "Oh yeah. This is going to be so good."

Chapter Ten

Danielle smiled as she moved around table after table with her tray of drinks held high over her head. It was another packed night at the club where she worked. Another night of fending off the customers that wanted to take her out. Another night of great tips.

Even though she didn't need the money, Danielle needed the human contact. Coming to Vegas and buying herself a home she could call her own wasn't enough. She wanted to live life and to do that she needed to act like everyone else. She was even thinking about taking a few college classes.

"Ah, sunshine," a regular customer smiled at her as he lounged back against the bar, "When are you going to leave this dump and come away with me?"

Danielle gave her order to the bartender and smiled at the man. "Toby, I've told you before. You're not my type."

"Yes, but I can be."

Danielle leaned a hip on the bar and smiled. One hand went to her hip that was barely covered with her short jean skirt and tank top. It was the dress code for the club. All the girls had to wear this black tank top that was tight and short, exposing her belly button. Also had to have a tight jean skirt that was at least a good five inches above the knees. It was something that Danielle didn't normally wear, but it brought home damn good tips from men like Toby.

"Toby, why don't you get out and find yourself a woman that will fall to her knees from your charm? Cause you sure as hell won't find her in this place," she said sweetly before she walked away.

"Hey Dannie!"

Danielle worked her way over to a couple of other waitresses. She grinned as a twenty was stuffed into her pocket by a guy as she walked by him. "You think they would get a life."

"Oh please!" Barb, a waitress Dannie's age said as she rolled her eyes, "They come in this place to grab our asses and get an eye full of our tits." She glanced around the room before she looked at Danielle, "Hey we're all going out for breakfast later. Want to join us?"

"Can't," Danielle grinned, "My brother has decided to come up for a visit."

"Back to work girls!" the bartender yelled.

Dannie shook her head as she went back to work. She was only a part time waitress so for the first time in months she was looking forward to the end of her shift, which was only four hours away.

Those four hours went by so slowly that Danielle thought she was going to scream. When two more waitresses finally came in and her shift ended Danielle thought she was going to kiss the ground. Parties were still going on in the club and it showed no signs of slowing down as she walked out the back door to her new jeep.

The drive to her house was a good forty-five minutes. Danielle wanted something that was away from the strip; something that had the peace and quiet that she seemed to long for the most, now that she was on her own.

When Danielle pulled into her drive she half expected to find a car there waiting for her. So it was a big disappointment to see no vehicle was waiting for her. Her first thought was that Paul didn't come after all, but then a light in her front room told her differently. Danielle never left a light on in her home when she wasn't there.

Danielle walked up to her front door with very tired feet. If it wasn't for the excitement of seeing her brother then her whole body would be dragging. Unlocking the door and stepping inside Danielle found that the one thing she wasn't expecting was a room full of flowers.

Roses of every color were scattered all over the tiny front room. Even red petals were scattered on the floor. Candles were also lit around the room, giving off a very romantic feeling.

"What the hell?" Danielle asked herself as she dropped her bag on the floor. Dannie's first thought was that Paul had a lady with him. "Paul, what are you up to?" Danielle walked up to a soft pink rose and closed her eyes to smell it. She smiled when she heard footsteps behind her, expecting to see her brother. She wasn't expecting what she saw.

"Hello, Dannie."

Nate stood in her tiny kitchen dressed simply in a snug pair of jeans and baby blue t-shirt. His hair had grown some since the last time she saw him, but Dannie found that he was still a hot sight to look at.

"Nate," was all she could say in a shocked, breathless voice, "What are you doing here?"

Nate saw the pain in her eyes and the tears that she suddenly worked hard at pushing back. He also saw the one and only woman he ever wanted looking like she was about to crumple to the ground.

"I came here for you," he told her simply, "I came here to be with *you*."

A single tear fell from one eye as she bit her lower lip, "Why?"

Her question tore at Nate's heart as nothing ever had. He heard the heart breaking within her by that simple word. He felt her pain as if it was his own, and wanted nothing more than to take it all away, to bring her into his arms where she belonged.

"I never wanted you to leave that night," he told her, stuffing his hands into his pockets. "I never wanted you to go."

"Nate, please!" she groaned, turning her back on him.

Nate rushed up to her, taking her firmly by the arms and forcing her to look at him. "This time you're going to listen to me, Dannie," he sighed in a harsh manner, "Damn-it! Don't you know what has happened here? Don't you care?" More tears fell from her eyes as she looked up at him. "Haven't you seen it, felt it?"

"I feel it so deep that it's killing me inside," she sobbed. "I die each night from it."

Nate relaxed his hold on her arms, but didn't let her go. Tenderness filled his eyes as he looked down at her face. "Then let's stop killing each other and live like I know we're supposed to."

"I don't fit…"

Nate stopped her with a gentle shake, "I don't want to hear any more of this bullshit about how you don't fit into my world! My world is what I make of it and it isn't anything but a pile of shit if you're not in it with me." He let go of her arms only to cup her face gently. "I refuse to follow in my father's footsteps and be alone. My mother loved him with all her heart, but he chose the money over her. I'm not going to do that." Nate let go of her face and went down on one knee before her. He looked up at her shocked face. All his love shown in his eyes. "Danielle Hughes. Marry me? I have never loved or needed anyone as I do you. Be my wife, my partner in life, my soul. Marry me?" He pulled out the small box that he had tossed to Paul. It was the same box he had been carrying around with him the night she walked out.

Danielle thought her eyes were going to pop out. Nate opened the box and what was inside it had her knees buckling. It was the blue diamond ring she had tried on at *Cartier's*. It was the large, square blue diamond engagement ring, the very one that she loved so much but worked so hard at hiding it.

"Marry me, Dannie?" Nate asked again, "Make me the luckiest man alive by becoming my wife.

Danielle was so speechless that she didn't know what to say or what to do. Her heart longed for this. Hell she even used to dream about it. But to have Nate on his knees with the ring asking her to be his wife was more than she ever thought would or could happen.

She started to laugh suddenly, which brought on even more tears. It also seemed to make Nate very uncomfortable, "Oh, my god!" she cried, "I don't know what to say."

Nate smiled but it was an unsure kind of smile. "Say yes."

Danielle nodded her head. "Yes."

Nate smiled brightly and stood up fast. His arms went around her body, picking her up from her feet and hugging her tightly as he swung her around. When he stopped, he looked her deep in the eyes and smiled.

"Right now."

"What?" she cried with shock.

"Let's do it right now."

"Are you out of your mind?"

Nate chuckled. "Damn right I am. I lost you once and hell will have to freeze over before I do that again." Nate placed her back on her feet but before he let her completely go he slipped the ring on her finger, kissing the fingers as he went. "A perfect fit and a perfect ring for you. Now where is a phone?"

"What do you need a phone for?"

Nate kissed her on the lips quickly. "Because, baby, we're going to a chapel in a limo, then a grand tour around the city that never sleeps. I want you as my wife as soon as I can."

Nate never gave her a chance to change her clothes. He called for a limo then went to work kissing her and holding her tightly. Once they were in the limo he told the driver to take them to the nearest chapel, then handed him a wad of hundreds for the rest of the night.

* * * *

"Do you, Danielle Margaret Hughes take this man to be your husband?" the old man asked Dannie.

"I do," she answered back.

"Do you, Nathaniel James Remington, take this woman to be your wife?"

"I do," he answered with a smile.

"Then by my power I declare you husband and wife. You can now kiss your bride."

Nate pulled Danielle into his arms and kissed her deeply. Keeping his lips on hers, Nate bent over and scooped her up in his arms. He smiled against her mouth as she squealed out in surprise. He carried her all the way out to the waiting limo.

"You are crazy!" Danielle laughed, pushing her tight jean skirt down as far as it would go.

Nate leaned forward. His hands went to her bare legs, pushing the skirt back up. "You have no idea."

Danielle looked at him as if Nate had lost his mind. She giggled in a nervously as he pulled her over his lap. It took Danielle a few moments before she understood what Nate was planning on doing.

"You can't be serious," she cried softly in shock, "Not in here!"

"Right here," he told her as he took hold of her panties, "Right now," he finished with a hard yank, ripping them off.

Nate kissed her hard and deep. His hands went down to cup her bare ass, pulling her even closer as he became instantly hard. Eight months he had been living in a state of hell alone. Four months he lay in his bed alone, thinking of her.

"I need you right now," he told Danielle against her lips as his hands worked at pushing her tank top up over her breasts.

While Nate was working on her top, Danielle took it upon herself to work on freeing Nate's hard cock. The moment her hands closed around the hard length, Nate hissed in pleasure. Nothing in his whole life ever felt this good. It was something he knew was going to last until he died.

Danielle didn't waste any time. She also felt the need to be as close to Nate as she could get. Taking all of the control she captured Nate's eyes while she slowly lowered herself onto him. With a smile in place she took him inside her.

Danielle put her hands up on the ceiling of the limo while Nate's hands cupped her breasts. She moved in short, power bursts that sent sharp sensations racing up and down her spine. Nate matched her movements. He bucked under Danielle just as hard, loving how she made his body come alive.

Nate watched her closely as she closed her eyes and rode him. The frown on her face told him she would orgasm soon. Two really hard thrusts had Danielle moaning in what sounded like pain, but her nails in his shoulder told him differently. Two more sharp thrusts and Nate was coming with her. Even though it was a short ride, it was a ride that he would remember until the end of time.

* * * * *

"If you don't get that very nice ass of yours to packing we are going to miss our flight," Nate told Danielle. He walked up behind her, wrapping his arms tightly around her body and smiling when he saw that she was staring at her wedding ring.

"We can't miss the flight," she chuckled back, "It's your plane we're getting on."

"True." He nuzzled her neck, holding her tighter. "But we still have a time to be on the plane."

Danielle sighed, resting her head on his chest. "Maybe I'm just not ready to go back and face the world."

"Too late to get cold feet now." He kissed her shoulder before he turned her around to face him. "You said I do. Remember?"

Danielle smiled faintly. "I guess I'm just afraid that you're going to wake up real soon and realize you made a big mistake."

Nate put his fingers over her lips. "Hush! I don't want to hear you talk like that. I didn't make a mistake. I made the best choice that I ever made in my life. And if the snobs back home don't like what I have done with *my* life, then they all can kiss my ass." He grinned. "I love you Dannie. I think I fell in love with you when you beat the shit out of one of my old girlfriends back in high school. You're never going to get rid of me, and if you even *think* about trying you will find that it will be one hell of a fight that you can never win."

Danielle smiled brightly. "I forget when it was that I fell in love with you." She brushed his hair from his eyes. "I just know that I have for so long that I still have to pinch myself at times to make sure this all isn't some kind of dream."

A twinkle started in Nate's eyes. He pinched her on the ass, chuckling when she yelped. "Does that help? I would hate for you to think this is some kind of dream."

"You are so funny," she said and laughed.

"I do try to be."

Danielle sighed as she leaned into him more. "Are you sure we can't stay here longer?"

Nate groaned, "I wish we could, but we can't." He pulled her out of his arms only to give her a slight push along with a swat to her ass. "Now, Mrs. Remington, get that fine ass of yours ready. I want to be home as soon as we can so I can get started on planning our honeymoon."

"Why don't we just stay here and call it our honeymoon?" she smiled over her shoulder.

"Because, my sweet," he gave her a wicked smile, "I want to have my complete way with you on this hot, white sandy beach I know."

Danielle gave Nate a sexy grin, and then dropped to the rumpled bed. "How about we stay here and you can have your way now?"

Nate chuckled, rubbing his chin. "If you don't get ready to leave in the next ten minutes, I'll have to carry you over my shoulder out of this room and through the lobby for everyone to see."

Danielle rose up on her elbows. "You wouldn't," she challenged back.

Nate leaned down, bracing his hands on the bed and keeping his body inches from touching hers. "Want to try me?"

Danielle bit her lower lip as she smiled up at Nate. Quickly and out of now where, she snaked her arms around his neck and pulled him down to her. She kissed him passionately, wrapping her legs around his body as much as her tight skirt would allow.

Nate let her have her way for only a few minutes before he pulled away with a smile on his face. "Nice try." He laughed when she dropped her head and groaned. "Now let's go and face the music."

"Fine!" she groaned again, "But if you get the cold shoulder from all of your business partners, don't say I didn't warn you."

Cold shoulder was not what happened at all. Danielle was shocked to find her mother and brother at the airport when they landed. Also a few co-workers, including Nancy, were waiting as well. All congratulated Nate and Dannie, and demanded they have some kind of party to celebrate the marriage. It was agreed, but not until after the honeymoon. Nate told everyone that he wasn't ready just yet to share his bride with everyone.

Three weeks later an article showed up in the paper announcing the marriage of Nathaniel Remington to Danielle Hughes. It was the most shocking thing to hit the stands since Nate was worth more than ninety million dollars. No one thought that he would get married at a young age and they sure didn't think he would marry a nobody. The only thing that seemed to stop many of the rumors was when people found out how passionate Nate was about his love for Danielle. He made it very clear to anyone that didn't approve of him or his wife they would not be welcomed into his world.

"So tell me how happy you are right now," Nate said to Danielle as they lounged in front of the fireplace. He handed her a glass of wine. They were both content, with bodies spent.

"I'm so happy that I can barely move," she moaned with a smile.

Nate chuckled. "I love it when you can barely move."

Danielle put her glass down and crawled up on his lap. She kissed him lightly on the lips. "I love you."

Nate hugged her tightly, burying his face into her hair. "God I love you, Dannie. And, if I had to, I'd give all of this up in order to keep you just like this."

"Oh, don't do that," she purred, "I want to take my mother shopping and plan on spending lots of money."

Nate smiled brightly. "Baby, if you do what you just did to me tonight every night, then you can spend all the money you want."

"Now that's a promise I can keep," she sang as she pushed him back down. "So let's get started on me keeping it."

The End

www.ingramcontent.com/pod-product-compliance
Lightning Source LLC
Chambersburg PA
CBHW020149180626
46810CB00004B/1804